Fear My Gangsta 2

Tranay Adams

Lock Down Publications and Ca$h
Presents
Fear My Gangsta 2
A Novel by *Tranay Adams*

Lock Down Publications

P.O. Box 870494
Mesquite, Tx 75187

Visit our website @
www.lockdownpublications.com

Copyright Fear My Gangsta 2

Lock Down Publications
Like our page on Facebook: Lock Down Publications @
www.facebook.com/lockdownpublications.ldp
Cover design and layout by: **Dynasty Cover Me**
Book interior design by: **Shawn Walker**

Stay Connected with Us!

Text **LOCKDOWN** to 22828 to stay up-to-date with new
releases, sneak peaks, contests and more...
Thank you.

Submission Guideline.

Submit the first three chapters of your completed manuscript to ldpsubmissions@gmail.com, subject line: Your book's title. The manuscript must be in a .doc file and sent as an attachment. Document should be in Times New Roman, double spaced and in size 12 font. Also, provide your synopsis and full contact information. If sending multiple submissions, they must each be in a separate email.

Have a story but no way to send it electronically? You can still submit to LDP/Ca$h Presents. Send in the first three chapters, written or typed, of your completed manuscript to:

LDP: Submissions Dept
Po Box 870494
Mesquite, Tx 75187

DO NOT send original manuscript. Must be a duplicate.

Provide your synopsis and a cover letter containing your full contact information.

Thanks for considering LDP and Ca$h Presents.

The Definition of FEARLESS

1.   Free from fear; as fearless of death; fearless of consequences.
2.   Bold; courageous; intrepid; undaunted; as a fearless hero; a fearless foe.

CHAPTER ONE
2011
Present night

Buzzzzz!

The huge metal door of the federal prison facility rolled back. As soon as there was enough room for a body to walk through the opening, thirty-six year old Davino strolled out wearing the exact same clothing he did when he'd went inside. An L.A fitted cap and a black Dickie suit. As he strode towards a big body Escalade truck, he couldn't help taking in the full scope of the huge vehicle. It was triple black with twenty-eight inch chrome rims which gleamed. He could tell the SUV had a rather large sound system because the loud music coming from it caused it to pulsate. Acknowledging this, Davino smiled broadly, thinking of how his homeboy, Buck, loved everything big from his cars to his women.

Davino walked upon the front passenger door of the Cadillac truck and opened it. As soon as he did he was smacked in the face by the sound MMG's *Self Made* album. Sliding into the seat, he slammed the door shut behind him and dapped up his man, Buck. Buck was a dark-skinned brotha that wore his hair in a short afro. He had a medium build and hands that were scarred from years of brawling in the streets. The man was a warrior, some may even say a gladiator, but all would agree he was a coldblooded killa. When Davino was out on the streets and running the show, Buck was his enforcer. All he had to do was point his finger and the nigga that had violated would be left bleeding where ever the fuck he was standing. It was safe to say that Buck was about his murder game.

"Welcome home, baby!" Buck greeted Davino with a big smile, dapping him up. A blunt was pinched between his fingers and the smoke from it was wafting around him.

He was in a brown long sleeve T-shirt which you could see the outlining of his wife beater under and blue jeans.

"Thanks, bruh. I thought I'd never be so happy to see yo' ugly ass face again." Davino cracked a smile.

"Fuck you, man." He grinned and pulled off, trying to pass the blunt to Davino.

"I'm good."

"You good? Nigga, yo' ass could smoke Snoop Dogg under the table before you went in, now you don't chief?" he asked, indulging in the blunt again as he steered the SUV.

"Yeah, man, shit's changed since I been away. I don't drink or smoke no mo'." Davino confessed. "If I'm gonna be the head of my own empire again, then I'ma do it with a clean and sober mind, you feel me?"

"Most def'. That's grown man shit." He busted a right at the corner.

At that moment, Buck's cellular rang and he switched hands with the blunt. Blowing smoke out of his mouth, he pulled out his cell phone and looked at the screen to see who was calling him. Seeing that the number was familiar, he answered the call and pressed the device to his ear.

"'Sup wit it?" Buck spoke into the cell phone. "I'm on my way now with 'em. Yep, we'll be there in a hot one. Peace." He disconnected the call.

"Who was that?" Davino inquired.

"The young homie, you know 'em…Reckless. Said he has you a welcome home gift and shit."

"Is that right?"

"Yep."

"If it's not pussy or food then it can wait, you already know what kinda time I'm on." Davino rubbed his stomach and grinned. He'd been thinking about all of the shit he was gone eat his last three months locked up. In fact, he'd been fasting for the past two days just so he could pig out on some shit. He couldn't make up his mind on what he wanted to eat so he said fuck it, and decided to get everything he could think of.

Buck's face turned serious and he said, "Trust me, Davino, you wouldn't want this to wait. As a matter of fact, it's something you been wanting to do since you were incarcerated."

Davino looked to Buck and Buck nodded. They'd just communicated to one another what they had in mind.

"Since it's that, food and pussy gone have to take a backseat." Davino's eyebrows slanted and his nose wrinkled up. He tightened his jaws and a vein twitched at his temple thinking about the punk-ass mothafucka directly responsible for putting him on lock for the past ten years.

"So, you want me to take you where he's at?" Buck looked back and forth between the windshield and his boss.

"Please, do." He clenched his fists so tight that his knuckles bulged. He busied himself by staring out through the window at the city streets.

***

Buck led Davino down into the basement of a crack house. Coming down the staircase, he could see the light shining in the darkness from the center of the room. He also heard the growling of a dog as it was mauling someone. The person that was being attacked tried his damndest to scream, but whatever was inside of his mouth was prohibiting it. Once Davino and Buck reached the landing of the basement they found a young man by the name of, Reckless. He was a rather short dude with a muscular body and short dreadlocks. His dark caramel skin displayed the tattoos that covered him from his neck down to his sleeves. He had thick eyebrows, a big pickle nose and big pink lips. There was also a gap between his two front teeth, and one was longer than the other. He'd probably rank number three in the world's ugliest dudes, but his reputation as a killa was fearsome.

"That's right, get his bitch-ass, boy, get 'em!" Reckless egged his pit pull on as he held firm to the chain he had him on. He was wearing a black bandana around his neck, a gray hoodie and red Dickies.

Reckless watched as his pit bull, who had its jaws locked on Lil' J's leg, shook its enormous head from side to side. The wild beast shaking its head caused Lil' J's naked body to fall down in the chair he was duct taped to. Lil' J's eyes were wide and full of fear. He looked down at the animal, hollering over and over again. The veins in his temples and neck bulged as he screamed in terror, trying to kick the dog from off his mangled leg.

"Grrrrrrr!" the pit bull shook its head violently, causing Lil' J to slide back and forth on the floor. The animal's mouth was covered in blood and blood was also dripping on the ground.

Buck and Davino stood by watching the pit bull maul Lil' J for a minute. Once Davino got tired of watching the show, he called for Reckless to stop. Seeing that his big homie was finally home caused Reckless to smile. He tugged on his pit bull's chain and commanded it to stop. The beast obliged him and returned to his side, sitting down. The dog looked around panting with blood dripping from its mouth.

Reckless took the time to chain his pit bull up to a radiator at the far corner of the basement. He then stepped to Davino and gave him a gangsta hug, patting him on his back. When they broke their embrace, Davino held him at arm's length and looked him over. It had been ten long years since he'd seen him. The young gangsta was twelve-years-old then, but now he was twenty-two with strong street ties and credentials.

"From a pup to a hound, huh?" Davino smiled further.

"That's right a big dog. And I got Buck to thank for showin' me the ropes." Reckless admitted. "Real shit, the homie groomed me to be the G I am today."

"Yeah, I heard how my young homie been out here ripping and tearing shit up. I thought you'd probably got too big for yo' Dickies and would wanna have to run the outfit yo' self. Thought I was gone have to come down here and get in yo' ass." Davino stood back and threw playful punches at the young wig splitta. Reckless bobbed, weaved and threw a couple back at him. They then hugged again.

"Welcome home, big homie!"

"It feels good to be back, fam." Davino patted him on his shoulder. He looked over to Lil'J and his face balled up with anger and his jaws squared. The vein at his temple bulged with hostility. "Excuse me," he told Reckless and stepped over to Lil' J, looking down at him. He didn't say anything for a minute as he looked at him, taking stock of his wounds. Reckless's pit bull had chewed on his face as well as the rest of his body. The poor bastard had bite marks covering him from head to toe. His normally tapered curly hair was wet with his own blood and sweat. He was shaking uncontrollably, and at that moment he had just pissed on himself. "Y'all sit this piece of shit up, man."

With their boss having given the order, Buck and Reckless sat Lil' J up in the chair. He sat there with his head bowed and shaking continuously. They then stepped back and allowed Davino to approach him. The first them he did was press his sneaker against Lil' J's testicles and mash down on them. Instantly, his head shot up and he hollered out in excruciation, but the gag in his mouth halted any sound from escaping. Once Davino lifted his sneaker from off his nuts, Lil' J was left looking him in his eyes. Tears welled up in his eyes and went sliding down his cheeks.

"You got the nerve to cry, you slimy mothafucka? You wasn't crying when you planted that bird in my truck and called them crackas on me! Yo' ho-ass wasn't crying then, now was ya?" Davino smacked him viciously, back and forth across his face. Sweat and blood flew from off his face and splashed on the floor.

Lil' J was Davino were brothas. Lil' J acted as his second in command, but he had bigger aspirations. Fuck being an underboss, he wanted to be the head nigga in charge, and the only way he could do that was with his brotha out of the way. Realizing this, Lil' J snuck the car keys off Davino one night when he'd gotten high and drunk at a bachelor party for one of their homeboys. He stashed a kilo of cocaine under the spare tire and called the police on him once he'd left the party. Davino was got popped with the kilo and was sentenced to a mandatory of ten years. While he was locked up, he gave his plug to his little brotha and let him run shit.

Lil' J had always seemed to be envious of Davino, but he didn't pay it any mind. He never thought in a million years his brotha would set him up, but something at the back of his mind was telling him otherwise. This was why he decided to sic one of the baddest bitches in the city on his brotha. She was a red bone with big tits and an even bigger ass, by the name of Suga. Suga had some fire head and her pussy was the truth. She had Lil' J's ass opened like a can of paint. Homie was tricking hard on little mama. He took her on shopping sprees, bought her a Benz, copped her *her* own little townhouse out in Manhattan Beach and even proposed to the bitch.

One night while pillow talking, Lil' J fucked up and told Suga how he'd set his brotha up. As soon as she left that morning, she dropped the news on Buck who then reported it to Davino. Although Buck and Reckless were ready to lay that nigga Lil' J down, Davino called for them to stand down. He didn't want anybody laying a hand on his brotha while he was locked up. As far as he was concerned, he was the one that had been wronged, so Lil' J was his problem to deal with. Davino had been waiting for his revenge for eight long years, and now, here was his chance to pay it back to the nigga that had stabbed him in the back.

"Yo'," Reckless tapped Davino and he looked at him. "I got somethin' for you behind the staircase, follow me."

Reckless and Davino disappeared into the shadows behind the staircase, leaving Buck alone with Lil' J. While they were gone, Buck pummeled his face with punches, sending sweat and blood flying from off him. Lil' J's head jumped back and rocked from side to side from the vicious punches which swelled him up worse and caused the cuts on his face to bleed more. Once Buck had finished beating on him, he was breathing shakily. Staring at the young man with hatred in his heart, he wiped his bloody fists on his pants.

"You a real piece of shit, you know that? I should pop yo' ass down here, but you deserve something worse than death." Buck shook his head and harped up some phlegm, spitting in Lil'J's face. The nasty glob splattered against his forehead, rolled and dripped off his brow.

Davino emerged from out of the shadows of the staircase shortly after Reckless. He was wearing a wielding mask and a blow torch. He activated the torch and a flame sputtered to life. The bluish yellow flame licked at the air, illuminating the mask that he was wearing. Davino slowly brought the flame towards Lil' J causing him to lean his head all the way to the side and dance in his chair. He was hollered something, but again the gag prohibited him from saying anything. Lil' J whipped his body from left to right as the flame neared him, making the chair he was in screech across the floor. The flame was about to touch his face when he pushed off the floor with the balls of his feet. The chair tilted to the left and slammed hard against the asphalt. Lil' J winced as he lay where he was on the floor. Looking up, he saw Davino bending down to cook the side of his face.

"Mmmmmmmmmmm!" Lil' J's eyes bulged and his mouth stretched wide open, showcasing all the cavities he had inside of his big mouth.

The flame of the torch sizzled and cooked the flesh on Lil' J's face, melting it like cheese. Davino brought the flame up and down the side of his face and neck, letting the fire singe his hair and burn his skin.

"Mmmmmmmmmmm!" he tried his hardest to scream through the gag, but it wasn't working. He continued to thrash around on the floor as the flame cooked him alive.

***

The Escalade truck pulled into the recreational center and drove around to the basketball court. Once it stopped, its doors opened and everyone hopped out, Davino, Buck and Reckless. Davino stood beside the truck's hatch with a big hammer and a tan sack of large nails. He watched as Buck opened the hatch. Together, he and Reckless pulled Lil' J's bloody, naked ass out and drug him over to the basketball court. The entire move Lil' J's head was bowed and he was moaning from his wounds. The entire left side of his head and face had been charred by the blow torch. His flesh looked like beef jerky. Once the fellas had taken him to the center of the basketball court, they were instructed by Davino to hold his arms down. They obliged him.

Davino got down on his knees and sat his fitted cap aside on the asphalt. He then took three of the nails out of the sack. He placed one against Lil' J's right palm, holding it there as he lifted his hammer high above his head. He held the hammer above his head a moment, and then he swung it downward with all of his might.

Ding!

The nail penetrated Lil' J's palm and blood flew. Lil' J's eyes stretched so far open they looked like golf balls in his eyes sockets. He screamed in bloody murder, with that pink thing at the back of his throat shaking.

"Ahhhhhh! Ahhhhh! Ahhhhhh!" Lil' J screamed louder and louder. He thrashed around but Buck and Reckless held fast.

"Gag this punk-ass nigga'z mouth!" A scowling Davino ordered, holding the nail and lifting the hammer above his head again. With the command given, Reckless pulled off the only sock Lil' J was wearing and crammed it inside of his mouth, holding his hand down over it.

Ding! Ring! Ping!

Davino swung his hammer down with great force, driving the nail further and further into Lil'J's hand. Lil' J screamed as loud as he could, but the gag muffled the sound that threatened to leave his mouth.

Dink!

The hammer swung downward again and pinned Lil' J's hand to the ground. Breathing shakily, Davino rose to his feet, with specks of blood on his face and shirt. Using the lower half of his shirt, he wiped his face and begun on Lil' J's other palm. Again, he placed the nail against it, holding it in place. He lifted the hammer again, and brought it down with all the might he could muster.

Dink! Dink! Ring!

Lil' J thrashed around, hollering aloud, but his efforts were useless. More blood flew, clinging to Davino's clothes and face. Buck and Reckless turned their heads so that the blood wouldn't get into their faces and eyes. Lil' J's eyes rolled to the back of his head. It looked like there were white Q-balls in his eyes sockets. His mouth quivered in agony.

"Disloyal-ass nigga, 'pose to be my brotha, but you betrayed me! You fucking Judas!" A furious Davino hollered aloud, spit flying from off his big lips.

Dink! Dink! Ring!

Each downward swing of the hammer forced the nail further and further into Lil' J's palm. His screaming had ceased and he lay there, letting Davino do to him what he willed.

Dink! Dink! Ring!

The hammer struck fast and angrily, until it finally pinned Lil' J's other hand to the asphalt. As he lay there going into shock, Davino picked up the last nail and moved down to his feet. He crossed his feet over one another and held the nail against them. He hammered the nail over and over again until Lil' J's feet were pinned and bloody.

"Look into that sack and gemme that crown, Buck." Davino told him. Buck fished a crown of thorns from out of the sack and carefully passed it to him. Davino took it and placed it over Lil' J's head. The pointy thorns that it was made of pricked his forehead and blood ran down his face. The blood that spilled outlined his brows, the side of his nose and both sides of his mouth.

Davino rose to his feet breathing hard, with his face shiny from perspiration. He wiped his face with the back of his hand and slipped his fitted cap back over his head. With Reckless and Buck by his side, he looked down at his brotha who he'd crucified.

"While I was locked up, I heard you said you was like Jesus to mothafuckaz in the streets. We'll now you get to die like 'em." Davino said to Lil' J hatefully. He then looked to Buck. "Hand me the sack and let's get the fuck from up outta here."

Buck handed him the sack and he dropped the hammer inside of it. He then slung the sack over his shoulder and carried it back to the Cadillac truck. He climbed inside of the SUV with Buck and Reckless getting in behind him. Buck cranked the big body truck up and drove off into the night.

Tranay Adams

CHAPTER TWO

Fear sat with his head hung and bound to an iron chair by rope. A dirty, yellowing light bulb hanging from a string illuminated him from above, flies circling it. The bulb flickered from time to time like it was threatening to go out. Fear's captor, a brown skinned man with a muscular build, stood off to the side, smoke wafting around him as he indulged in his habit. He observed him as if he were a wild animal inside of a cage at the zoo. The man dropped a cigarette at his sneaker and mashed it out, blowing smoke out of his nostrils and mouth.

"Hey, wake up!" He yelled at Fear. When he didn't get a response, he swung his hand across his face.

Smack!

"I said wake your black ass up, nigga!" Spittle jumped from off his lips, palm stinging from the attack. He continued his assault, only more viciously.

Smack!

Smack!

His nostrils flared and his chest rose and fell rapidly. He bored down at his shorter man with contempt. Closing his eyes and taking deep breaths to calm himself, he disappeared into the shadows of the darkened basement. When he returned, he was toting a tin bucket full of water. He stopped before Fear, cocked the tin bucket back, and splashed water into his face. Fear's head shot up and he gasped for air.

"Haaaa!" He sounded like someone had held his head underwater and waited until the last minute to let him up. Water cascaded down his face as his eyelids fluttered and he took in his surroundings. Once his vision finally came into focus, he got a good look at the cat standing before him.

"Fuck are you, man?" Fear asked with an attitude, his voice resonating throughout the space.

"I'm Detective Broli."

Fear tried to move, but the rope held him fast. He looked down and saw that he was bound tightly to an iron chair. When he saw this, his brows furrowed and wrinkles formed across the beginning of his nose. What the fuck is this? He wondered what the hell he was restrained to a chair for.

He looked up and asked, "What's this shit about?"

"You," Broli answered. "I've been watching you these past few years. You've made an insane amount of money pushing crack, kingpin. That's tax free money, so the Feds aren't seeing one red cent of that. So I figure why don't I step in and play Uncle Sam? From now on, I want fifty percent of your take. Your workers, your lawyer fees, anyone else who may have put the lean on you, that's your business. Their pay comes outta your end. I don't give a damn, fuck you pay me. We understand one another?"

Fear threw his head back laughing. I mean, he actually had tears forming in his eyes he was laughing so hard.

"Hahahahahaha, ooooh, shit," Fear came down from his laughter, chuckling. "You should do stand up, my nigga. You're the next Red Foxx. Whoo! Me? Getting muscled for my empire? That will be the day a nigga applies the pressure game on me and I fold. Fuck I look like nigga?" He harped up a glob of phlegm and spit on his sneaker, glaring up at him like What the fuck you gone do?

Broli frowned and clenched his jaws, looking down at the nasty goo on the side of his sneaker. He kicked his foot until most of the phlegm went flying across the way. He felt himself getting angry, but he quickly caught himself, a sinister smile across his lips making him resemble the devil himself.

"What do you look like you ask?" Fear watched closely as he popped the trunk of his car and removed a briefcase. Closing the trunk shut, he advanced in Fear's direction and sat the briefcase on his lap, popping its locks. He lifted its lid and removed a stack of black and white photographs. Slamming the briefcase shut, he laid the photos on top of it and went through them, one by one.

Broli looked up at Fear who was still smiling from his laughing earlier. Both of the men were smiling, but it was the crooked detective that held the trump card.

"Let's see how long you're wearing that smile of yours, asshole."

With each photograph that Broli revealed, the smile on Fear's face grew smaller and smaller until it had vanished. Fear felt his heart slide deep down into the pit of his stomach and wither like a dying leaf. The black and white photographs were of Fear participating in the murders of The Bluudlow Brothas, The Untouchables, and purchasing large shipments of weapons. Broli had him by the balls and was squeezing them, tighter and tighter. "I get the feeling that you've changed your mind."

Fear sat there with his head hung, shaking it. He shoulders rose and fell as he took deep breaths, thinking long and hard.

"Fuuck, man, shit!" he screamed and stomped the floor. Afterwards, he shut his eyes briefly and took a couple more deep breaths, calming himself. "Alright," He began, looking up at the shady badge defeated. "How you wanna play this?"

Broli put his fist to his mouth and cleared his throat. "I'm glad you asked." He patted his leg and pulled up another iron chair, sitting down. "Fuck what I said earlier, that's too much hassle. I've gotta 'nough drug dealers on my payroll. What I want from you," as he spoke he jabbed him in the knee with his finger for emphasis. "is one million dollas in cold cash."

"One million dollars and I walk?" He looked him square in the eyes for any signs of his lying.

"One million dollas and I'll even burn this here evidence in front of you." He held up the photographs.

"How do I know you're not lying? You've gotta gimmie yo' word."

Broli's face twisted with anger and he leaned forward. "Let's get something straight, mothafucka, I've gotta 'nough dirt to lock you away for three life times." He held up three fingers. "You aren't in any position to bargain. I ain't gotta give you notta goddamn thing!" He dropped the photos on top of the briefcase and sat back in his chair, folding his arms across his chest. "So what's it gonna be, kingpin? You gon' un-ass that cash or am I gon' have to slap some cold cuffs on yo' ass?"

"If I give you this money, that's it, I can go?" he asked to make sure, searching his eyes for truthfulness once again.

"One million dollars and you're a free man. And the evidence is all yours." He patted the briefcase.

"Okay. I'll take you where I stashed it, cut me loose."

"Alright then," Broli began, picking up the machete from the floor, getting upon his feet. "Just so you know, if you try anything, I'ma use this big bastard to behead yo' mothafucking ass. Got that?"

"Loud and clear, killa," he spoke with a no nonsense attitude. Broli stepped behind him and relieved him off his bondages, with one swift swipe of the machete. The severed rope hit the floor and Fear rose to his feet, massaging his wrists.

"The doors open. Get inside of the car." Broli pointed his machete at his whip. Fear went to move too fast for him and he drew his piece from its holster on his hip. The swift motion caused him to look over his shoulder, eyebrow raised. "Slow ya roll now."

"Relax. I ain't going nowhere." He retreated to the car with the dirty detective by his side. Broli forced him inside of the car on the front passenger side with his gun pressed into his ribs. After passing his hostage the keys, he cranked up the engine and pulled off.

Fifty five minutes later

Italia sat on the couch watching TV. The blue illumination of the screen shone on her face as she held the remote control in her hand, changing the channels. She was bored as hell and couldn't wait until her man got home. Hearing the keys jingling at the front door, she sat up straight and slid her gown off of her shoulder. A sexy smile apprehended her luscious lips and she turned toward the door, sliding up her nightwear so that her boo could get a good look at her inviting thigh. She was hoping to entice him and possibly get some dick that night. Her pussy had been twitching the past couple of hours and she was in dire need of some of that thug passion.

The front door came open and the smile fell from her lips seeing Broli standing behind her dude. As soon as he saw her, he pressed his banger further into Fear's back and gripped the collar of his shirt tighter. The look he shot her was like Scream and I'm going to do this nigga right here. She read him like a text message and complied. The beauty wasn't about to do anything that would jeopardize the life of her lover.

"Babe, what's going on?" She inquired; worry was etched across her face.

"Everything is going to be okay, sweetheart, he'll be outta here in no time. I just gotta pay 'em off so he can go."

His eyes darted to their corners at Broli. "Ain't that right, Big Dawg?"

"Sho' ya right." His dangerous eyes focused on Italia, wishing she would do something foolish so that he could blow a hole in her man's back. He pulled a pair of handcuffs from his back and tossed them on the floor at Italia's bare feet. "Cuff yourself to the guard railing of the staircase." Once he was done watching her do as he'd ordered, he led her guy upstairs where he claimed he had the million dollars stashed. They found themselves inside of the master bedroom. Gun still on Fear, Broli was ordered to dump the pillows from out of the pillowcases. He was planning to use them to carry all of the loot he would be given.

"Open up the safe, nigga! Come on, you taking too fucking long!" He shoved him peevishly.

"I got this, chill out."

"Chill out?" He gave him the evil eye. *Whack!* He smacked him across the back of the skull with that steel, dropping him down to a knee. He grimaced, holding his hand to the back of his dome. When he glanced at his hand he saw that it was masked with blood which meant that a gash had opened up on his head. "Talk back again and I'ma put one in yo' spine, lil' nigga! Now find that safe and pop that bitch open!"

Gritting in pain, Fear opened the closet door and parted the clothes hanging upon the rod, granting a clear path to a solid steel, digital safe that was as tall and as wide as a door. When Broli seen the safe, he smiled and stared at it like it was love at first sight. "Open her up." He nudged Fear who was still holding the back of his head wincing. He punched in the combo and the door made a thunk, coming ajar. When he pulled open the door, Broli almost nutted in his jeans. There were eight shelves and there wasn't one of them that didn't have money on it. Every stack accounted for was secured by a rubber band. It was more than a million dollars here, two or three maybe, but definitely more. Broli passed the pillowcases to Fear and he started filling them up, making sure that he'd given him a million dollars. Once he was done, he sat the lumpy pillowcases down just outside the closet.

"There you go, a mill, now get the fuck out my house," Fear spoke to him like he wasn't shit.

"There's been a change of plans." When he said this, Fear instantly became furious, clenching his fists. "I want it all, every last dolla."

"That wasn't the deal," he said through tightened jaws.

"Well, I'm breaking it." *Whack!* Broli struck him on the side of his head, dropping him down to his knees. "I don't wanna see or hear about chu even touching crack, ya hear me? That isn't your hustle anymore, find yourself a new one 'cause should I catch wind that you're still out here doing you, I'ma kill you, ya understand?"

"Fuck...fuck you!" Fear winced down on his knees, rubbing the side of his head.

Broli kicked him in the ribs and when he doubled over, he was rewarded with the butt of the gun slamming into the back of his skull. Fear hit the floor on the side of his face snoring, having been knocked out cold.

An hour later

"Uhhh...uhh." Fear groaned and grimaced coming out of his unconscious state. His head was pulsating and his vision was blurry. He felt the back of his head again and came away with dry blood. Slowly, his vision came into focus and he looked up at the safe. Suddenly, he forgot about his headache when he saw that he had been cleaned the fuck out. There wasn't a dollar left inside. It was as clean as a whistle. Fear grabbed a hold of the safe door and pulled himself to his feet. He gave the safe another scan just to make sure that he wasn't overlooking anything. Once he saw that he was indeed broke, he slammed the door of the safe and kicked it violently. "Shit! Shitt! Shittt!" He swung on air, hands looking like blurs while in motion.

"Alvin! Alvin!"

"Italia?" He looked alive hearing his name being called. He darted out of his bedroom and stopped at the head of the steps. Looking down, he saw his lady still handcuffed to the guardrail. "Hold up, baby." He hurried down the staircase and headed into the two car garage where he grabbed a saw. When he raced back inside of the condo, he saw the rod that his girl had been cuffed to until it came loose. As soon as she free, she threw herself into his arms and he hugged her lovingly. "You, okay, babe?"

"Yes, are you?" She looked up into his face.

"Nah," he shook his head no, glassy eyed and shit, "That dirty mothafucka cleaned me out." He balled his hand into a fist and it bulged with veins. Gritting, he slammed his fist into the wall behind him, knocking a hole in it.

"It's okay, I got like, three hundred thousand saved you could flip…"

"I'm through with that game."

"What chu mean?" She frowned.

Fear went on to explain to her what had happened that night between he and Broli as well as the law that he'd laid down about his hustling.

"Well, what're you gonna do?" She questioned, caressing the side of his face.

Fear shut his eyes and took a deep breath, blowing out hot air. He felt defeated, but what could he do? His head was on the chopping block. Suddenly, he remembered something else that he'd always been good at doing. His eyelids peeled apart and he locked eyes with his soul mate.

"I got it, I got it." He said in his eureka moment. "Throw on something; I need you to take me somewhere."

"Okay." Italia got halfway up the staircase before he was calling after. She turned around to him raising an eyebrow.

"Get whatever money that chu have stashed, alright?"

"Alright." She continued up the staircase and disappeared inside of the master bedroom.

Fear circled the couch and plopped down. Leaning forward, he rested his elbows on his knees and steepled his hands underneath his chin in contemplation. Closing his eyes and exhaling, he realized that he didn't have a choice in the matter he had to do what he had to do. The action that he was about to take wouldn't be too far a leap from his current occupation. It wasn't like his hands weren't already stained in blood. Shit, he was already condemned to spend an eternity in hell, so it wasn't like he wasn't like anything he did now would change the route in which his soul was heading.

"Okay, I'm ready," Italia called from the staircase as she came running down them.

"You got my guns?" Fear stood to his feet.

"Yeah." She nodded a little out of breath, holding up the gun case that housed both of his Glock .9mms.

"Good. Let's get the fuck outta here." He headed for the door removing his cell phone from his pocket. Italia had just pulled out of the garage when the person he was calling picked up.

"Sex, I need you to meet me at Hahn's in two hours. I don't have time to explain, just be there, family," Fear spoke into his cellular. "I love you, bro, peace." He disconnected the call and slipped his cell back inside of his pocket. Afterwards, he took a deep breath and slid down in his seat.

"Hahn's?" Italia asked to make sure.

"Yeah, later though, first we're hitting all my stashes houses," Fear told her. Then he went onto inform her about the move he was about to bust. While he was telling her exactly what it was that he was up to she didn't seem to have bat an eyelash. "Look, if you with me cool, but if you not, I understand 'cause this is a different level of the game. With that being said, where is yo' head at with it?"

"I'm down for you to the very end."

"I salute cho gangsta."

Fear interlocked his fingers with hers, brought them to his lips and kissed them tenderly. He smirked at her and laid his head back against the headrest, staring out of the window as they continued their journey. Where they ended up next would completely change the course of his life. Nonetheless, it was a move that he felt had to be made.

***

Big Sexy sat in the backseat of an unmarked car talking on his cellular phone. The hood of his hoodie protruded slightly over his head, casting a shadow that kept most of his face in hiding. The only identification of it being him was his signature thick, nappy beard which he'd occasionally comb with a natural fork.

"Alright, my nigga, I'll see you there. I love you, too, peace." He disconnected the call and took a deep breath, running his hand down his face. Stashing his cellular inside of the pocket of his hoodie, he continued to comb out his beard. "This shit is all fucked up, man; I can't believe I did this shit. Snitching? That ain't what G's do." He sucked his teeth and shook his head shamefully, having become what he despise the most.

"Aye, aye, look at me." The man called over his shoulder, looking at him through the rearview mirror from the driver's seat. The husky man's eyes met his through the reflection of the mirror. "You did what chu had to do, you hear me? You didn't have a choice. It was either him or you. Shidddd, if I was in your shoes, I woulda did the same thing. Hell, for that matter, I'm sure he would have to." He looked out of the driver's side window, watching the streets through the tinted glass.

"You think so?"

"You bet cha motha's ass. This game don't have no loyalty, homeboy," he told him reassuringly, eyes still focused on the outside. "You can love her but she won't love you back, believe that."

"I can dig it." Big Sexy nodded his understanding. He knew what he had done was some foul ass shit, but at least he was going to walk away a free man after all of the deception. It was a cold world. If it wasn't for this cheese eating mothafucka, Broli wouldn't have gotten the photographs of all of the dirt that Fear had done.

"What did our friend say?"

"He's headed to Master Hahn 's."

"Hahn ?" The mysterious man's brows furrowed. He narrowed his eyes as he tried to figure out exactly where this Hahn stood in Fear's life, but he came up with nothing.

"He's a martial arts teacher," he informed him, still combing out his beard. "He's been training him since he was a lil' nigga."

"What chu think he's gonna do there?"

"I don't know. I mean, nothing much. Hahn is an old ass man; there isn't much that he could want with him."

"Right, right, right," he nodded his head continuously.

"I did my part, can I get that now?"

"Yep, a deal's a deal," his voice changed as he leaned over into the passenger seat, opening the glove box. He pulled out a file and passed it to the backseat. Through the rearview mirror he watched Big Sexy, who was his confidential informant, flip through the documents inside of the file. "Satisfied?"

"And these are the original documents?" He questioned, trying to make damn sure. He'd sold his best friend out for what was inside of that folder and he wanted to make sure he'd gotten his just due.

"Yes, all of the originals, just like we agreed," he assured him confidently.

"Good, I'm outty." He opened the door and hopped out. Crossing the parking lot of the park he was inside of, he set fire to the pointed end of the file and watched the flames devour it. Seeing half of it engulfed, he tossed it inside of a trash can as he passed it, glancing back over his shoulder. "Bitch-ass nigga." He pulled the drawstrings of his hoodie and enclosed it around his head, tying it up. Next, he stuck his meaty hands inside of his pockets and went on about his business.

Back in the unmarked car

"Bitch-ass nigga." Broli laughed, picking up the extra file that was lying on the front passenger seat. He'd taken out this one along with the one he'd given Big Sexy. The crooked mothafucka made duplicates. "Hahahahahaha!" he laughed heartily, slapping his knees. Afterwards, he wiped the tears from the corners of his eyes, sat the file aside and cranked up his vehicle, driving off.

Meanwhile

Fear pushed open the door of Hahn's store. The bell hanging over the door chimed as he crossed the threshold. Japanese Folk music played softly in the background. He turned to the bronze life size statue of Buddha and rubbed its belly for luck. This was something he'd done every time he'd entered the store. Fear turned away from the statue and inhaled the inviting scent of Jasmine incents. Closing his eyes and tilting his head back, he took a good whiff before taking in the full scope of the establishment. The place was dimly lit and its shelves and display cases were fully stocked. It was like a liquor store, boutique, weed clinic and antique store all in one. Come to think about it, the place resembled that store that Gizmo was bought at in the Gremlins movie.

Hearing someone approaching at his left, he looked to find Hahn approaching from the backroom. He advanced in his direction taking puffs of an antique pipe that looked like it had been stolen from a museum of Asian artifacts. At first Fear thought it was tobacco, but the aroma expelling from the pipe gave him second thoughts. A whiff of its stench confirmed it for him. It was Kush. The old man was definitely smoking some high quality, top-shelf shit.

"What is it that I can do for you, Alvin Son?" He and Fear bowed to one another. After the pleasantries were exchanged, the old man brushed past him, in step towards the door. Fear stated his business as he watched his teacher lock the door and turn the *Open* sign over to its *Close* side.

"I need you to teach me any and everything you know about killing," he told him straight up, looking him square in the eyes. "I need to obtain the skills you had when you were putting niggaz on their backs for Gustavo. Train me, Master, train me to be an assassin like you were."

Hahn took the pipe from his lips and blew out a cloud of smoke. "Why do you need these set of skills? Tell me, Alvin Son, are you in some kind of trouble?" He paced the floor as he listened to Fear. His head was tilted downward so that he'd be focused on the floor, occasionally taking draws and causing smoke to waft around him like he'd just done a magic trick.

"So I've gotta leave the game behind and search for another means to run a checkup. So I figure why not do something I familiar with?"

"Hmmm," he stopped in his tracks, sucking on the end of the pipe and stroking his beard with an unkempt hand. "I'm afraid I can't…"

He was stopped short once Fear dumped the Reebok duffle bag's contents out on the counter, stacks upon stacks of money came tumbling out. Hahn looked pleased when he saw all of the racks that had spilt on the glass counter top. The old man couldn't help but wonder how much it was scattered out before him.

"That's a hunnit and fifty grand for your troubles. And don't tell me you don't need the money. You've come down with cancer, right? When we talked I could tell that you were worried about leaving them with a lil' bit of nothing. Well, here's something. If you train me then it's all yours, every penny of it. That I assure you."

Hahn shut his eyes, took a very deep breath and then exhaled. Peeling his eyelids open, he went to deny Fear but felt a stinging inside of his chest. He grimaced and coughed into his palm. Taking his hand away, he saw the sticky blood there. A length of red saliva hung from his lip to his palm.

"Ah, shit." He curse having seen the blood, the cancer had begun its work on him.

"Master Hahn, I…" A worried Fear lifted his hand and approached, but his teacher raising his hand stopped him.

"I'm fine, I'll be okay." He looked at the pipe in his hand and became enraged, throwing it aside. Next, he wiped the blood off on his clothing. "Okay, you've got yourself a deal."

"Master Hahn, I think you should…"

"I did not ask for your opinion!" His eyebrows arched as he growled. "Now do you, or do you not want this deal?"

Fear took the time to calm himself down, closing his eyes for a moment and slightly nodded. Once he peeled his eyelids back open he said, "Yes, I do."

"Alright then, we leave tomorrow at dawn, deal?" He extended his scrawny old hand, his bony fingers lingering in the air.

His protégé firmly grasped his hand, shaking it. "Deal."

Hahn gave Fear the address and the time to meet him the next morning. The master and the student shook hands and bid one another farewell.

***

Fear and Italia decided to spend the night at a hotel. They ordered room service, showered and got dressed for bed. As they lay in bed watching television, Fear hit up Big Sexy.

"Yo', Sex," Fear began when his right-hand man picked up his call. "Change of plans. Grab an ink pen and a piece of paper. I want chu to write this address down" he went on to give him the address of the location he was supposed to meet Master Hahn. "Be there 'round six. I let chu know everything you needa know once you touch the turf. Nah, nah, everything is good. We'll chop it up in the A.M, family. I love you too, my nigga. Peace." He disconnected the call and sat his cell phone on his dresser.

Fear scooted up against Italia so that his dick was pressed against her ass and wrapped his arms around her. He kissed the back of her head and stared ahead at nothing, like she was. The blue light coming from the screen of the television partially illuminated them. For a minute they didn't say anything to each other. They were too busy with their own thoughts. Finally, Fear decided to break the ice.

"One year. That's twelve months were not going to see each other. That's a long while." Fear said aloud of the time he'd spend with Master Hahn training. "That's gone kill me, babe. I don't know how I'm gone manage, a nigga may go crazy up in those mountains."

Italia didn't say anything for a minute. She continued to lie on her side, caressing his hand with her thumb. Suddenly, she turned over in bed to him and said, "You're right. Twelve months is a long while, so let me give you something to remember me by."

Italia cupped Fear's face and kissed him passionately. His strong, masculine hand ran up and down her arm as they made out. They turned their heads from side to side as they shared a sensual kiss. Once she pulled back and looked into his eyes, she could see all of the love he had for her.

For a minute, Italia and Fear stared into one another's eyes as he caressed her cheek with his curled finger. Holding his wrist, she kissed his palm tenderly, making sure to keep eye contact with him the entire time. Afterwards, Italia straddled his muscular body and leaned forward; planting kisses as soft as flower petals down his chiseled chest and eight pack abs. Fear pushed his head back into the pillow and shut his eyelids, gasping as her tongue circled the head of his dick. Holding his dick with one hand, Italia sucked on his nut sack and watched pleasure cross his face. Her pussy became wet seeing she was pleasing her man sexually. She dragged her warm, moist tongue under his penis and started sucking it.

"Ahhhh, shit!"

Fear winced and trembled all over. He held the back of Italia's head as she bobbed up and down on his grown man. He made an ugly face as he looked down at her handling her business. He found himself watching her as she was watching him. The sight caused his dick to get even harder.

Her head bobbed faster, her slurping and sucking noises filled the room. The nasty sounds mingling with the show playing on the television. Her hot saliva ran down his dick and coated his balls. He grabbed a handful of her hair and started fucking her mouth, sliding in and out of it as if it was her pussy. As she continued to suck him off, she reached between her legs and parted her pussy lips, rubbing on her swollen clit.

Italia's eyes rolled back as Fear fucked her mouth, looking her straight in the face. He went faster and faster, making her gag loudly. More of her hot saliva poured down his engorged meat. Fear pulled his dick out of her mouth and ordered her to stick out her tongue. He tapped his dick against her tongue and teased her with it, sliding it back and forth across her mouth. Italia took his hand away and grabbed his dick, sucking it long and strong, driving him crazy. When she finally pulled his grown man out of her mouth, it made a loud suction sound. Wanting some dick, Italia threw the sheets off of Fear and climbed on top of him. She leaned forward, reached back and grabbed his member. She lifted her ass and eased down slowly, guiding the head of his penis towards her slick, pink tunnel. She hissed feeling her man's meat fill her to capacity.

"Goddamn, bae," Italia uttered with her eyelids closed and licked her lips.

"Goddamn, bae, what?" Fear asked, looking up into her face and interlocking his fingers with her fingers.

"Yo' dick…yo' dick feels so good." She stammered, bringing her buttock up and down upon him.

Italia rode Fear hard and fast, building up a sweat and a steady rhythm. She came over and over again riding him, bouncing up and down. Her rapid movements caused her hair that wasn't matted to her face to bounce. Her cries of lust, love and passionate filled the air. Fear's manly moans and groans weren't far behind.

"This my pussy, baby?" Fear asked, holding her perfectly sculpted breasts in his hands as she came up and down upon him.

"This always been your pussy, bae. Even when we weren't official!" she whined. "Is this…is this my dick?"

"All yours boo, can't no other bitch get this! This all you!" he swore, meaning that shit.

"I love you so fucking much, babe. I'ma miss you."

Tears slowly began to roll out of the corners of her eyes.

"I love you too, boo. I'ma miss yo' ass too, but I'ma be back." He gave her his word, eyes glassy.

"You promise?" she asked, looking down into his eyes while still riding him.

"On my dead homies!" he vowed.

"I want you to bust in this pussy!"

Once Italia said this, Fear pulled her down against him and wrapped his arms around her. He then pulled his legs in and spread them open. Now his thick, long dick could be seen inside of her gooey pussy hole. He drove his hardness in and out of her, creating a creamy white lather. She begged him for mercy because he was killing the pussy but he wouldn't stop. He kept at it, pounding her the fuck out. Before he knew it, the veins on his penis bulged and his nuts swelled. He held his breath as he pumped feverishly, sweat rolling down his face. His eyelids were squeezed shut and his jaws were clenched. Suddenly, he threw his head back and busted inside of her. His warm semen oozed out of her hole as he continued to hump her, emptying his nuts inside of her womb.

Fear kept humping Italia until he had nothing else to give. His legs went flat on the bed and Italia laid the side of her head against his chest. They both breathed shakily, having had powerful orgasms. Staring up at the ceiling, he held her tight in his arms and kissed the top of her head. It wasn't long before they both had drifted off to sleep.

Tranay Adams

CHAPTER THREE

The sun was on the rise as Fear drove out to the mountains where he was going to be training. Taking hold of the steering wheel with one hand, he picked up his cellular from where it was charging on the console and speed dialed Gustavo. The phone rang three times before the person he was calling picked up.

"Hello?" Gustavo answered the telephone groggily

"'Sup, G?"

"You tell me. You're the one that woke me out of my sleep."

"My bad, but this can't wait."

"What's the emergency?"

Fear was silent for a minute before he finally answered him. "I'm out, G."

"Out? What do you mean? What's going on? Is this cause for concern?"

"Nah, it's all good." Fear assured him. "I guess you can say I had what you may call a spiritual awakening."

"So, that's it, huh? You just gone walk away from everything you've built?"

"Yeah."

"Alright then, adios, mi amigo."

"Peace." He disconnected the call and sat the cell phone back down.

Fear looked to Italia and found her smiling at him. He smiled back at her and they kissed. She then took his hand and interlocked her fingers with his fingers. After kissing his hand, she looked out of the window and watched as the sky slowly began to change color.

***

It wasn't long before Fear and Italia were pulling up to their destination. Finding themselves at the bottom of the

39

mountain, they hopped out of their car and made their way around to the grill of it. Fear leaned up against the car with his arms wrapped around Italia's waist. Her arms were wrapped around his neck and she was staring into his eyes. They made out like a couple of teenagers at a drive-in theater. Hearing someone driving up, they looked up the path and saw an Avalanche truck headed their way. The truck pulled up behind Fear's ride and the engine was murdered. The driver's door came open and Big Sexy hopped out, Timberland boots landing onto the graveled ground. He slammed the door shut behind him and made his way over to his right-hand man.

"Yo' what's up, my nigga? What chu wanted to see me about?" Big Sexy inquired after exchanging daps and hugs with Fear.

"I'm out." Fear told him straight like that.

"What chu mean?" he pulled his sagging jeans back upon his ass. His brows were wrinkled. At that moment, he couldn't help thinking if word had traveled back to him that someone was snitching on him.

"I mean, I'm done with this shit, Sex. I'm done with drugs. It's time to make a change, you Griff me? This shit right here," he jabbed at the ground, referring to the crack game. "Has far too many risks, family."

"Nah, man," Big Sexy shook his head. He was now standing with his arms folded across his chest. "This don't sound like my ace I'm talking to right now. You sounding scared, but I know that ain't chu. Yo' mothafucking name Fearless, so I know ain't shit got chu spooked."

"You can call me what chu wanna, but I know when to throw in the towel." Fear reasoned. "If I keep at this shit then I'm bound to get caught up fighting the Feds. I ain't tryna go out like that, my nigga."

Big Sexy looked to the ground and took a deep breath. It was then that he knew Fear didn't know anything about him running his mouth to Broli, because if he had, he'd already put a bullet in his head. "If you walking away, then what chu plan on doing from here on out?"

"Murder game, my boy," Fear walked to the rear of his vehicle and popped the trunk. Holding it open, he reached inside and grabbed his Puma duffle bag.

"You mean, you gonna be a hit-man?" he made his hand into the shape of a gun.

Fear slammed the trunk shut and turned to his main man, taking a deep breath, he said, "Yeah. That's why I'm here to see Master Hahn. He's gonna train me to be a proficient killer."

Big Sexy massaged his chin and nodded. He then looked up and slapped hands with his right-hand man, saying, "Yo', man, if you like it I love it."

"Appreciate that." Fear tapped his fist to his chest. "You won't me to hit up the plug and tell 'em to deal straight witchu now or what?"

At that moment, Big Sexy stared into his best friend's eyes, trying to decide whether or not he was going to tell him everything that went down between him and Broli. Feeling that it would be in his best interest to just keep his mouth shut, he decided to let the conversation play out.

"Nah, my nigga, if you out then I'm out," Big Sexy told him. "Ain't no way I'ma keep thangs going without chu. We were a team. I'ma just find something else to get into. You feel me?"

"I feel you, Sex." He slapped hands with him again. "If you need anything, I want chu to holla at me, dawg. You know you my man, so I always got chu faded with everything. You know how we do."

"Fa' sho." Big Sexy said. "How long you plan on being up here training and shit though?"

He asked the question and then looked up at the stone steps of the mountain.

"One year, and then I'm out."

"Okay, hit me up sometimes."

"No can do," Fear shook his head. "I won't have any internet or cell phone access the entire stretch... Master Hahn's orders."

"Alright then, I'll see you in a year then."

"Twelve months." Fear told him.

"Twelve months." Big Sexy responded and hugged his brotha from another mother. They broke their embrace. The giant patted him on his shoulder and bid him and his woman a farewell before trekking back to his Avalanche truck. He jumped in behind the wheel of the SUV and cranked it, backing up and then driving off.

Fear stared at the back of Big Sexy's enormous truck as he drove off. He watched as his friend threw his hand out of the window and held up two fingers. Fear returned the gesture and turned his undivided attention to his lady, Italia.

"You been so quiet, I forgot you were even here, girl." He smiled and she smiled back.

"I didn't want to interrupt you and your homeboy's conversation." She responded as he pulled her into him. He was holding her by the waist and staring into her beautiful eyes.

"You could have. You know you got it like that, lover."

"Oh, do I?" she asked surprised, tracing his jaw line with her manicured fingernail.

"I thought you knew."

"Well, I do now." She leaned forward, kissing him deep and passionately. When they broke their lip lock, they stared into one another's eyes for a minute. When they done this, time seemed to stop and the world appeared to have stopped spinning. In that time, the only people that existed were the two of them. The love between them was at an all time high. They could feel one another's auras and they were very imposing. Their love was a force to be reckoned with. In fact, the only thing that could ever break their bond was them.

"I'll see you in twelve months, beautiful." Fear tilted Italia's chin upwards and looked into her eyes.

"Twelve months." She nodded. "I'll be waiting."

"You better be." He cracked a grin.

"Talk that shit, big daddy." She smiled and accepted his kiss on the lips.

Looking up, Italia saw someone at the very top of the stone steps. She couldn't make out whoever it was face, so she held her hand above her brows and took a closer look. Fear frowned, looking back and forth between her and whoever she was staring up at. She finally dropped her hand to her side and turned to him.

"That's Master Hahn up there. I think he's waiting for you."

Fear looked up at the first stone step and confirmed that it was the man that was going to train him to kill professionally. "I'm sure he is. I better go."

Fear hugged and kissed Italia again. He then held both her hands up to his lips while staring her in her eyes, kissing the backs of her hands tenderly. She smiled and watched him begin his journey up the stone steps. Italia kept her eyes on her man for a minute before jumping behind the wheel of her car, cranking it up and driving off.

Once Fear had seen his lady off, he went about the task of climbing those long ass stone steps.

***

When Fear finally made it upon the mountain he was drenched in sweat. The collar of his shirt and under his arms was darker from perspiration. He was crawling on his hands and knees, huffing and puffing out of breath.

Looking upon Master Hahn, he tried to pull himself together as best as he could. It took some time but he finally made it upon his two feet. Once he did, he rested his hands on his hips and leaned his head back, trying to catch his breath.

"Goddamn!" Fear wiped the beads of sweats from his forehead with the back of his hand. His chest inflated and deflated with every breath he took. He was exhausted. The stone steps he climbed gave him quite the exercise. "I'ma have to lay off the blunts, gotta young nigga 'bouta die up here."

"That's the least of your concerns at this time, Alvin Son." Hahn said, standing before his apprentice with his weight leaning against a staff. His other hand was held behind his back, like he was hiding something.

"Yeah, I already know, you're gonna work my black ass to the bone." Fear threw the duffle bag down to the ground. He then yawned and stretched, hearing his bones crack and reset themselves. "Well, I tell you, Master Hahn, I'm as tired as a runaway slave, but I'm more than up for the challenge."

"Good, good, that's very good." Hahn told him. "Because starting now, I will have to kill whatever you are today in order for you to be reborn into what you need to be in the profession you've chosen to…" Right then, Hahn broke out into a bad coughing fit and smacked his hand over his mouth. His body shook as he continued to cough and gag. When he took his hand from his mouth he had blood in his palm. The cancer was slowly eating away at him. "Ah, shit." He wiped his bloody mouth and palm off on the sleeve of his garbs.

Worriment crossed Fear's face and he went to attend to Hahn, but the old man held up his hand, stopping him dead in his tracks.

"I'll be fine. You don't have to worry about me." he told him. "We have a year of training to complete, so we better get started."

"But..."

"But nothing," Hahn cut him short, talking to him as if he was his son. "A deal is a deal. Now, put on these weights and this backpack." He spoke of the backpack and the ankle weights beside him. It wasn't until he pointed at the items with his staff that Fear noticed them.

Fear's forehead creased as he wondered what he was going to be doing with the weights. Nonetheless, Fear strapped on the ankle weights and slipped on the backpack, which was exceedingly heavy. He then buckled the backpack across his chest and looked at Hahn.

"Jesus Christ, how much do these things weigh?" Fear gritted and adjusted the straps of his backpack.

"The backpack is loaded with two-hundred and fifty pounds in stones while the ankle bracelets are twenty-five pounds apiece." Hahn started coughing again, but this time he pulled out his handkerchief and coughed into it. He didn't bother to see if he'd soiled it with blood again. He just stashed the handkerchief within the recess of his garbs.

"What am I suppose to do with all of this shit now?" Fear winced, feeling the weight of the backpack.

"While you're wearing the weights, I want chu to try to catch it." Hahn told him with a no nonsense attitude.

Fear looked around confused, face balled up. "Catch what?"

With the question posed, Hahn nodded to the chicken that was hanging up in the tree. Fear glanced up at it and then back to his teacher, who was pulling a dagger from out of the confines of his robe. The sun's rays kissed off the dagger and a gleam swept up the length of it. He threw the dagger and it whizzed through the air hastily, looking like a silver blur. The dagger sliced through the hook and the cage fell to the ground, busting the lock on the cage's door. The door fell open and the chicken came out, clucking and flapping its wings. It went running off into the distance and leaving feathers in its wake.

"What are you waiting for? Go catch it. Your training has begun." Hahn told him.

"Shit!" Fear went running after the wild chicken.

Hahn stared at his student's back as he ran off into the trees of the mountain top. A smirk formed on his lips and he folded his arms across his chest. It looked like Fear was moving in slow motion. The amount of weight he was carrying was definitely holding him back, but that was the idea. After this exercise, Fear would be moving faster than he'd ever been.

"You better hurry up, Alvin Son, 'cause that's for dinner." Hahn laughed. His laughter then turned to coughing and he placed his hand over his mouth. After his coughing fit he looked to his palm and saw blood. "Shit." He said, knowing that he was another day closer to death. The cancer was too far along for him to get treatment, so he opted to spend the rest of his days training his favorite student. Afterwards, he figured he'd go back home to die in bed, with his granddaughter and her daughter by his side.

Taking a breath, Hahn wiped his hand off on his clothing and retreated to the cabin.

11:30 P.M

Hahn sat on a log tending to a black pot of cooking rice with a large wooden spoon. The black pot hung from a cast iron tripod over a camp fire prepared by the Master himself. The golden orange flames cooking the rice illuminated Hahn's face. Once he figured he'd finished tending to the rice, he sat the spoon aside and picked up a canteen. He removed the top and took a swig. Hearing rustling among the cluster of trees on the mountain top, Hahn leaped backwards, high into the air. Swiftly, he drew his dagger from his other sleeve and threw it where he'd heard the noise coming from. Still holding the canteen, he landed on his bending knee and stared in the direction he'd thrown his lethal weapon.

The dagger was halfway buried into the ground at Fear's booted feet. Fear was covered in sweat, scratches and dirt. The shirt he was wearing was tore around its collar and he was missing his left sleeve. There were also tears in the legs of his jeans. He was still wearing his backpack full of stones and the ankle weights. He was breathing shakily. Oddly enough, he looked exhausted yet happy.

"Damn, you almost got me in my foot." Fear looked down at the dagger. He then pulled it out of the ground and wiped the dirt on it off on his jeans. Next, he held up the wild chicken his master had sent him after, upside down. The chicken was just as dirty as he was. He'd twisted its neck until it snapped so it was hanging awkwardly. The bird flapped its wings sporadically, sending its feathers flying everywhere, and then slowly falling to the ground. "Look at what I got...dinner." He smiled from ear to ear, but seeing that his master wasn't as happy as he was erased the expression from his face. He lowered the flapping bird at his side and looked at his master as he headed towards him, casually strolling. "Well, I thought you'd be proud of me for catching this crazy ass bird."

Hahn wore a stern expression on his face as he made his way in his student's direction. Finally, he stopped before him and placed his hand on his shoulder. Looking Fear in his eyes, a smile stretched across his face and he held the canteen out for him to take it.

"I am proud of you, but I have one question for you." Hahn said as he squeezed Fear's shoulder affectionately and watched him drink from the canteen thirstily, spilling water down his chin.

Fear brought the canteen down from his lips and wiped his chin with the back of his hand. Looking at his master, he said, "What's up?"

"What the fuck took you so long?" Hahn looked him square in his eyes.

"Man, I oughta knock you out!" Fear chuckled and threw playful jabs at Master Hahn. The old man doubled over laughing and smacking his knee. He stood upright and wiped his tears of laughter away with his curled finger. Coming down from laughing, he said, "I'm just kidding, Alvin Son. I had faith in you all along, which is why I took the liberty to prepare the rice." He outstretched his hand towards the pot of rice.

Fear smiled knowing that his master had so much confidence in him.

"I figure once you wash up, you could pluck that bird and I can show you how to properly gut 'em. How does that sound?"

"I fucks with that." He dapped him up.

"Alright then, come on, Alvin Son." Hahn killed the fire with a bucket of water he'd placed nearby. He then pulled an oven mitt over his hand and took the black pot from the tripod. Next, he walked towards the cabin with Fear bringing up his rear.

Fear pinched his shirt and held it up to his nose, sniffing it. His face balled up having inhaled the foul stench, and he said, "Man, I stink something awful."

"Yeah, God awful." Hahn frowned and fanned the stench from his nose.

"Awww, you cold, Master Hahn." Fear chuckled.

"I'm just keeping it one hundred, as you youngstas say."

***

Broli came out of the corner liquor store stashing a small Hennessy bottle inside of his leather jacket. He removed the plastic wrapping from his pack of Black & Milds. He opened the pack and took out one of the slim cigars, sliding one between his lips. Stopping, he slid the pack into his jacket pocket and whipped out his Zippo lighter. Snapping the lid off the shiny metal lighter, he was about to produce a flame with it when something caught his eye. Looking up, he saw a crackhead copping rocks at the corner directly across the street from him. As soon as he got his fix, another crackhead approached the slinger and copped. Then came another, another, and then another. Once the slinger had made his last sell, he looked up and spotted Broli clocking him.

The crack slinger scowled and pocketed the money he'd made from the sell. He then lifted up his shirt and showed the chrome handgun in the waistline of his sagging jeans. "Keep it pushin' up the block, homie! It ain't nothin' to see here!" Broli lifted his hands up in surrender and went on about his business. "Ol' punk-ass nigga!" the crack slinger spat off the curb and went back to waiting for smokers looking to cop their next hit of poison.

Making his way towards the parking lot where his BMW was waiting for him, Broli produced a flame with his lighter and licked the tip of his cigar with it. Once the tip turned ember, he took a couple of puffs from the end of it and blew out a cloud of smoke. Rounding the corner of the liquor store, he bumped into a shabbily dressed crack fiend with an unkempt afro and a torn collar.

"Say, G," the crack fiend began, scratching underneath his chin. "You think I can get two nicks for this hot eight dollas?"

Broli switched hands with the Black & Mild. He then pulled his chain from the inside of his shirt and let it drop. When it extended its full length his shield snagged on it and rocked back and forth. Once the crack fiend saw this, his eyes bulged and his mouth dropped open. He could have pissed on himself seeing the gold shield before his eyes. The shield gleamed under the dim lights of the liquor store's parking lot.

"Oh, my—my bad, officer," The crack fiend took off running, looking over his shoulder to see if Broli was following him, but he wasn't.

Broli shook his head and continued towards his Beemer. He opened it with his remote control and pulled the door open. He slammed it shut once he slid in on the soft leather driver's seat. Having stuck the key into the ignition, he was about to turn it, but then he looked through his black tinted window. On the opposite side he saw that same crack fiend copping his fix from the slinger that had flashed him his gun earlier. Broli then looked straight ahead, taking casual pulls from his cigar as he massaged his chin, thinking. The smoke of his Black & Mild wafted around him like it was alive.

There's a lot of money to be made in the crack game. I fucked up letting that nigga Fear off the hook. I shoulda followed my first mind. I coulda had that mothafucka pushin' crack for me while I kicked my boots up and collected. Sure I may be taxin' a few cats out here doin' they thing, but what they kickin' in to me is peanuts compared to what a kingpin like Fear could bring in. Damn! Broli took another pull from his cigar and polluted the interior of his vehicle with more smoke. *Wait a minute! I still got his homeboy in the bag though,* he popped open the glove-box and grabbed Big Sexy's file. Shutting the glove-box back, he sat the file on his lap and opened it up.

As soon as he did, he came face to face with Big Sexy's mug shot. An evil smile etched across his lips.

"You, my fat friend, are gonna make me a ton of fuckin' money." He said, blowing smoke down at Big Sexy's mug shot and smiling again.

***

The way Big Sexy saw it, if Fear was leaving the game then so was he. What the fuck did he look like hustling knowing Broli was going to be watching his every move, nine times out of ten? He planned on packing everything he needed and cleared out his safe. Next, he was going to hop his ass on the next flight to Connecticut. He figured he'd go legit and open him up a Burger King or Family Dollar store. He knew with a business he could launder his dirty money and make it legitimate.

Big Sexy stuffed the last of his clothing inside of his suitcase, slammed the lid shut and locked it. He slipped the strap of the duffle bag over his shoulder and picked up both of his suitcases. He made his way out of his bedroom and into the living room, heading for the front door. Once he reached it, he turned around and gave the house one last look over before unlocking the door. As soon as he pulled it open he came face to face with Broil. He had a wicked smile across his face and his teeth clenched a toothpick. Big Sexy took a deep breath and lowered his head in defeat. This was because he already knew that the grimy-ass nigga had something else in store for him.

"Well, damn, big man, you don't look so happy to see me."

"That's 'cause I know that if you here, it spells bad news for me." Big Sexy frowned. He hated that mothafucka, and he would pop his ass, but he knew he'd get the gas chamber for murdering a cop.

"In this case, not necessarily." He claimed. "I came here to talk dollas."

"I gotta few stacks stored away, if you want that I can…"

"Nahhhh," Broli shook his head. "I ain't talkin' 'bout that loot you sittin' on. I'm talkin' 'bout the paypa we stand to make with you runnin' Fear's operation."

"Fear's gone. I'm shutting that down."

"Nah, you not shutting shit down."

"But he told me…"

"I don't give a fuck what that nigga told you, fat man. You don't do shit 'less I tell you to, is that understood?" Broli looked him dead in the eyes with a tightened jaw that displayed his bone structure.

Big Sexy mad dogged him and clenched his fists tight. He wanted to bust him in his mothafucking mouth, but he knew it was in his best interest to keep his hands to himself. Not only could the crooked mothafucka have him thrown under the jail for the dirt he had on him, but he could smoke him right then. He was positive that he'd pull out on him before he could grab his gun.

When Big Sexy didn't respond, Broli scowled and stepped closer to him, saying, "Did you hear me, nigga? Don't make me come up off my hip now." As soon as he said this, Big Sexy looked to his holstered handgun on his hip. Both of his hands were resting on his hips, and his right hand was right by his gun. He could pop him before he fucking blinked, so Big Sexy knew he'd better watch his mouth.

Big Sexy squeezed his eyelids shut and took a deep breath to calm himself down. "Yeah, I hear you."

"Good, boy," A smiling Broli patted him on the cheek like an Italian mob boss would have. "Now, I want chu to continue to run Fear's operation."

"That's all fine and dandy, but how in the fuck am I gonna run his shit? I don't have the loot I need to cop, and he sure as hell didn't introduce me to his plug. I'm fucked out here in these streets unless I get my hands on a nigga that can deliver me some top of the line cocaine."

"Don't worry about the coke, I got chu faded, big dawg," he patted him on his shoulder and squeezed it, smiling.

"Oh, you the plug?"

"Nah, I ain't Sosa, but I can get chu all the bricks you need. That won't be a problem." He assured him. "I gotta C.I that gives me an elephant's nut load worth of intell' on different fools around the city that's handlin' weight. I'm talkin' about major, major weight. I figure I could rob them faggots and drop the coke in yo' lap so that you can flood the streets. That way we ain't gotta worry about kickin' in no dough for the drugs. Whatever we make will be all profit from here on out, you feel me?"

Big Sexy stared down at the ground as he massaged his chin, thinking on everything that had been said to him by the crooked law dog. He then looked back up into his eyes and said, "Yeah, I feel what chu saying, it all makes sense. But I gotta question though, *boss*."

"Shoot."

"What's my cut in all of this?"

"Yo' cut, huh? I'll tell you what, my man. I'm notta greedy mothafucka. Your cut is twenty percent."

"Twenty percent?" Big Sexy's brows furrowed. "That's fucking peanuts, man. I'm gonna be doing all the ground work out there in these streets." He pointed at the door.

Broli stepped so close to Big Sexy's face that he could smell the nicotine and donuts on his breath. "First off, you lower yo' mothafuckin' tone when you addressin' me, homie. I ain't none of them lil' busta-ass niggaz in the streets who were working for you and Fear. I'ma mothafuckin' gangsta with a badge, or have you forgotten?" he pulled out his chain and let it fall. It snagged on his gold police shield and rocked from side to side. "I could pop yo' big fat pastrami sandwich eating ass with a hundred eyes and camera phones on me, and still get away scot-free. You understand me, huh? Huh, bitch?" he grabbed Big Sexy by the back of his neck and squeezed tight. The pressure caused what felt like a knife to stab him at the back of his spinal cord. He howled in pain and dropped down to one knee. He tried to grab Broli's hand, but he squeezed even harder. This action caused Big Sexy to drop his hand at his side.

"I got it, man. I got it." Big Sexy gritted in pain.

Broli released him and watched as he rose to his feet, rubbing the back of his neck and frowning.

"Now back to what I was saying," Broli continued with what he was saying earlier. "As a boss you will find me fair yet firm. You'll get all that's coming to you and a lil' bonus from time to time. On top of that, you'll be moving around with immunity. I'll see to it that you stay off my people's radar, just keep the murdering to a mothafucking minimum 'cause my homies gone come looking for answers if too many bodies come popping up. And when that happens, some mothafuckaz are gone have to go to jail. There won't be any ifs, ands or buts about it. Someone will have to pay a debt to society should too many folks come up smoked."

"Is there anything else I needa know?"

Broli passed him a cellular phone and said, "I'm the only one to have the number to that there jack. You don't give that bitch out for nothing. You use it to communicate with me and only me. Do I make myself clear?"

"Crystal."

"Now, if you'll excuse me, I'm gonna see about getting you your first shipment of cocaine. Have a good day." Broli tipped his cap to him and smiled. He then turned on his heels and made his way out of the door.

CHAPTER FOUR
The next day

Hahn walked towards a tree toting a chair and some rope which was looped around his shoulder. Fear followed him closely behind wondering what he had in mind. He found himself stopping shortly behind him as he sat the chair down and removed the rope from around his shoulder. He watched as his master tied the rope into a noose and threw it over the tree's branch. Hahn then tied the other end of the rope around a nearby tree. Afterwards, he stood upon the chair and pulled the noose down, tugging on it. Once Hahn was sure that the rope was secure, he jumped down from the chair. He then stepped before Fear smacking dirt from the palms of his hands.

"Uhhh, what's supposed to happen now?" Fear asked, looking up at the noose as it slightly rocked from side to side.

"I'm gonna loop the noose around your neck, and then take the chair from underneath your feet."

Fear angled his head and looked at him like he was crazy. "You mean you gone lynch my black ass, like you part of the Klan?"

"Yes." He nodded. "But not to kill you, I only want chu to look Death in the eyes and smile...laugh even. You see, to be a killa. One must not be afraid of anything, not even death." Hahn said as he walked around Fear with his hands held around his back. He then stopped on the side of him and gave his shoulder a manly grip. "Are you up for the challenge?" he looked him square in his eyes.

"Yes." Fear answered reassuringly. He wanted his master to know that he was willing to go to great lengths in order to succeed in his training.

"Good." He patted his shoulder and climbed on top of the chair. Afterwards, he motioned for his pupil to climb upon the chair beside him. Once he did, he looped the noose around his neck and bound his wrists behind his back with a bandana. He then stepped back down to the ground.

This is fucking nuts, what the fuck did I just agree to? Fear thought as he looked above and saw length of the rope that was around his neck as well as the branch it was hanging from. He then shut his eyelids and swallowed the ball of nervousness in throat.

"Okay, on the count of three I'm going to snatch this chair from underneath you, alright?" Hahn asked. A nervous Fear nodded and took a deep breath. "Okay. One. Two," he snatched the chair out from underneath his feet before the count of three, taking him off guard.

Fear's body hurled toward the ground, but the rope snatched him back up. He swung from side to side, eyes watering and legs thrashing. All he could hear was his heart thudding inside of his ears.

"Death is unexpected." Hahn looked up at Fear, struggling upon the rope. He stayed focused on him as he talked. "You wanna be a killa, then you need to accept the fact that death will come for you any time, any day and any place. You don't get to make an appointment, that merciless son of a bitch creeps up on you and it's your time to go."

Hahn watched as Fear danced on the rope. His eyes bulged and his mouth trembled.

"Gaaaaaah!" Fear gagged and blinked his watering eyes repeatedly, wincing.

The rope was like a pair of hands tightening around Fear's throat. He felt a ring of fire as the rope slid up his neck, burning it. Tears spilled down his cheeks and he clenched his jaws, displaying the muscles in them. Veins bulged at his temples and his neck. The veins on his shoulders, pecks and arms became pronounced as well.

"Do you see him? Do you see…Death?" Hahn asked as he stared up at Fear, hands behind his back.

Fear looked down at him. Right before his eyes, Master Hahn transformed back and forth to the Grim Reaper, flames dancing all around him. The scenery of the mountains became the atmosphere of Hell. Fear saw several demons and people screaming in agony that had been sentenced to eternal damnation. They all looked like they were in excruciating pain as the hottest of fires cooked their flesh, causing it to peel.

"Yes, I—I see him." Fear struggled to say, with the rope strangling him.

"Laugh at him. Laugh in the face of Death." Hahn urged him.

A slight smile formed on Fear's face. The veins that covered his face and body looked like they were about to explode. The smile on his face spread wider and wider, until he finally let out what sounded like a chuckle. As soon as he did, Hahn drew his dagger and threw it at the rope. The dagger spun like a helicopter propeller and sliced through the rope. Once the rope was severed Fear plummeted to the ground and landed hard on his side, wincing.

Hahn picked his dagger up from the ground and raced over to Fear. He sliced the rope that restrained Fear's wrists behind his back. He then twisted the cap off his canteen and aided him in drinking some water. Once he'd gotten enough water, Fear gulped in air and continued to breathe shakily.

"I did it—I did it." Fear told him.

"Yes. You did. You did good, Alvin Son. You did really good." Hahn assured him, smiling.

***

Broli's informant's information paid off. He and his squad came off like a couple of fat rats in a cheese factory.

Them niggaz was sitting on one-thousand bricks of raw cocaine. The kilos were in the back of two delivery trucks. Broli and his squad didn't even have to bust a single shot. They rolled up in that mothafucka five deep and as soon as the transporters saw their machine guns and badges, they bowed down and did whatever the fuck they were told.

Broli strolled down a line of men at his feet that were lying on their stomachs on the ground. Their mouths were gagged and their wrists were bound behind their backs with zip-cuffs. They struggled to get free of their restraints but their efforts were useless. There wasn't any chance in hell they were getting out of their bondages, and even if they did they'd be cut down by machine gun fire by Broil's men.

"Well, let's take a look at the merchandise, shall we?" Broli said to the men at his mercy. He then switched shoulders with the strap of the compact machine gun he had in his possession. Afterwards, he grabbed hold of the dangling strap on the delivery truck and pulled himself upon the bumper of the vehicle. He unlatched the lock and pulled the shutter of the transporting vehicle open. Inside there were several vases wrapped in cellophane.

Broli grabbed one of the vases and jumped down to the ground. He slammed the vase down and it exploded into pieces. Using his machine gun, Broli rifled through the cellophane and the broken pieces of the vase, until he found a neatly wrapped package. He picked up the package and smiled victoriously, looking around at all of his men. "Here we go, boys. The prize we've been looking for."

Some of Broli's men exchanged greedy smiles while other's high fived each other.

"Let's see what we got in this tight lil' package," Broli slung the strap of his machine gun over his shoulder. He then pulled out a big ass hunting knife; it twinkled once the sunlight kissed off of it. He then stabbed the package and slit it upwards, spilling cocaine. Broli dabbed his finger into the powdery substance and rubbed it around his gums. Instantly, he felt a numbness surrounding his mouth, like he'd been given a shot of Novocain. "Just like we thought, boys, co—mothafuckin'—caine…good shit, too."

With that having been said, Broli tossed the opened package into the back of delivery truck beside the rest of the vases. Next, he walked over to the side of the vehicle and picked up a red gas-can. He then locked eyes with his men and gave them a nod. Knowing what he meant by this gesture, the men pointed their machine guns at the men lying bound at his feet and opened fire on them. The restrained men were being massacred; blood and brain fragments were flying everywhere. Some of the blood and brain fragments splattered on the pants legs of the executioners, but they didn't pay it any mind, they kept on firing until all movement among their victims had ceased. Once the men had finished shooting their machine guns wafted with smoke. They ejected the spent cartridges from their automatic weapons and smacked in fresh ones, putting new rounds into the heads of their machine guns.

Broli instructed a couple of the men to drive the trucks back to the location they'd discussed before the lick. He then doused the dead men with gasoline. While he was doing this, the rest of his men were climbing inside of their vehicles and preparing to leave. Broli led a trail of gasoline towards the van he was going to ride shotgun in and dropped the gas-can on the spot. Jumping into the passenger seat, he pulled out his Zippo lighter and sparked up a Newport. He blew out a cloud of smoke and tossed the lighter onto the flammable liquid.

Froosh!

A line of fire ripped up the trail of gasoline and all of the dead bodies went up in a burst of flames. Right after, Broli slammed the door shut and signaled for the driver to pull off. The van pulled off while the fire was mingling with the gas-can. Abruptly, the gas-can exploded and a cloud of fire filled the background of the fleeing van.

That night

"Yo,' why the big homie just up and left the game like that?" Gunplay asked of Fear departure from the crack game. He was sitting across from Big Sexy in the patio of a Mexican restaurant. They were seated at a white table that was shaded by an umbrella.

Gunplay was a tall dude with an almond hue. He had thick eyebrows, a thin mustache and bushy chin hair. There was a black mole just below his right eye. He was considered attractive by traditional standards, but the aura around him screamed thug; most of the time he wore blue and rocked a blue bandana on his head, Juelz Santana style. At twenty-years-old Gunplay was the youngest wig splitta of Fear's crew.

"I don't know, man." Big Sexy shrugged with a jaw swollen with food. "Nigga, told me he was threw and he was leaving it all to me."

"Just like that, huh?" Gunplay raised an eyebrow. "You think that nigga witnessed a miracle or some shit and he turned to the cloth?"

"Fuck if I know." He grabbed his beverage and sat up straight. "Look, Gunplay, I'm holding the keys to this shit now. How I came by it? I don't know nor do I give a fuck. Shiiiiit, the way I see it. If a nigga give you the pink slip to a Bentley, you don't go asking him why he's giving you the shit. Hell, as long as that mothafucka paid for, hop in that bitch and drive. You feel me, homie?"

Gunplay nodded in agreement and took a sip of his beverage. "Yo,' you put hands on them tacos. You want a couple more?"

"Nah, big dawg, I'm good." He wiped his mouth with a napkin and balled it up, dropping it on the paper plate of what was left of his tacos.

"You sho? It's on me." Big Sexy said.

"Well, shit, since it's on yo' dolla, hell yeah." Gunplay grinned and rubbed his hands together greedily.

Big Sexy chuckled and reached inside of his pocket, pulling out a thick bankroll. He peeled off a dead face and dropped it on the table top. "Get me two of them shits, too. And another rice drink."

"Fa sho'." Gunplay picked up the hundred dollar bill and stood to his feet. He then made hurried footsteps to the window of the ghetto restaurant.

A sharp whistle from across the street stole Big Sexy's attention. He looked and saw someone standing in front of a midnight blue seven series BMW. Homie was dressed in a leather jacket and Timberlands, laces hanging loosely. The dude smiled and motioned him over, but Big Sexy wasn't budging. For all he knew that mothafucka could be looking to blow his head off.

"Come here, my nigga. Lemme holla at chu!" Homie said through his hands which were cupped around his mouth.

"Fuck is you?" Big Sexy asked, pulling his gun out underneath the table.

"B." he responded.

"B?" the giant ran the street name through his mental rolodex, trying to place the face with the name. That's when it dawned on him that B must have been short for Broli. "What the fuck is that nigga doing here? If niggaz see me with him, I'ma be food in these streets." He said to himself.

"Here you go." Gunplay came back with the food and drink, sitting them down on the table top. He looked at who

Big Sexy was talking with and his brows furrowed. "Yo', who is that nigga?"

"Uhhh, I don't know, but I'm 'bouta find out." Big Sexy picked up his beverage and made his way across the street, looking both ways. Once he finally made it to Broli, they dapped one another up and exchanged pleasantries.

"'Sup, man? I gotta tell you, this ain't a good look for me."

"What chu mean, big man?" Broli's forehead crinkled and he twiddled his toothpick at the corner of his mouth.

"Nigga, you One Time. If any street niggaz see me out here witchu, my name ain't gone be worth shit." He told him straight up. "Now if my name is tarnished, how the fuck you expect me to make moves out here? Ain't nobody gone wanna fuck with me. I'll be branded a snitch!"

"Damn, nigga, calm down 'fore you blow a gasket!" he placed his hand on the giant's shoulder. "I just came down here to tell you yo' first shipment is in. One thousand kilos." He tossed the keys to the place he'd stored the kilos to Big Sexy and he caught them.

"One-thousand birds? Goddamn." Big Sexy said impressed. He had a lot of weight on his hands, but he was sure he could move it all. There wasn't any doubt in his mind that he could handle it.

"Here's somethin' about me that you may not know. I don't fuck around when it comes to gettin' paid." He assured him. "Money talks and bullshit walks one-thousand miles."

Big Sexy nodded his understanding. "So, where do I go to pick the shit up?"

"There's a storage unit out in Gardena. Here, lemme give you there business card. I grabbed one there when I paid for the unit." Broli reached inside of his leather jacket and pulled out the self storage business card, passing it to Big Sexy. He told him the storage unit's number and pass code was on the back of the business card. The giant took the card, glanced at the unit's number and then slipped it inside of his pocket. "The work is inside of the vases, which are all wrapped in cellophane."

"Good looking out."

"No sweat." Broli dapped him up. "I'll be in touch."

The crooked law enforcer slid in behind the wheel of his BMW and fired it up. He then pulled off with Ice Cube's *Rhymes like weight* pumping from his luxury vehicle's speakers.

***

Once Broli had left, Big Sexy retreated back to where he'd been eating with Gunplay. They sat back down at the table and continued eating. Big Sexy tried to chop it up with him, but the young nigga didn't seem receptive to his conversation. He face stayed in his plate until they were both done. Afterwards, they hopped into Big Sexy's truck to leave. The drive to the storage unit was awkwardly silent, with Big Sexy occasionally glancing in Gunplay's direction. The expression on his face was rather solemn so he couldn't read it, but he knew something was up, he just didn't know exactly what.

"So, who was dude back there?" Gunplay inquired, throwing his thumb over his shoulder in the direction they'd just came from.

"That was my potna, he was just tryna see where he could get some good weed from?" Big Sexy lied.

"Oh, yeah?"

"Unh huh," He nodded, turning the stereo up. He continued driving and bobbed his head to the music.

While he was busy paying attention to traffic and the music, Gunplay pulled his handgun from off his hip. He then jammed it into Big Sexy's side causing him to wince.

The giant looked back and forth between his young homeboy and the windshield, wondering what the fuck was going on.

"Yo', what the fuck is up?" lines formed on Big Sexy's forehead.

"Nigga, turn that bullshit off and pull into the alley up ahead." Gunplay nodded to the alley coming up on his right. Big Sexy turned off the music and did what he'd been told.

"Now what?" Big Sexy asked. He'd just pulled inside of the alley.

"Turn the car off."

Big Sexy did what he'd been told and looked to Gunplay, saying, "What the hell is this about?"

"Yo,' homie back there, the weed smoker."

"Yeah, what about 'em?"

"He's a mothafucka narc, nigga busted my ass when I was a juvie."

There was silence as Big Sexy stared ahead. His heart was beating so hard the sound of it flooded his ears. He could feel his palms grow sweaty as he tried to figure out what to tell Gunplay. He knew that his answers had to be good; otherwise the young nigga would blow his head off.

"I know that look, cuz. So if you 'bouta tell me a lie, I'm fits na blow a hole in yo' side. Have them boys up in the 'spital fixing you witta shit-bag or something, you feel me?" he emphasized by pressing his gun further into Big Sexy's side and causing him to wince in discomfort.

"I guess the only way outta this is the truth, huh?"

"You mothafucking right!" he scowled harder and adjusted himself in his seat, leaning closer to him. If Big Sexy didn't come clean with what he believed was the truth, then he was going to leave that front seat a mess.

Big Sexy took a deep breath and went on to tell his story. "Alright, the nigga you seen me back there chopping it up with was a narc. He's also my new plug, since Fear's plug ain't fucking witta nigga."

"Why cuz ain't fucking witchu?"

"Man, that paranoid mothafucka only wants to deal with Fear. That's the only one he trusts." Big Sexy told him. From the look on Gunplay's face he could tell he believed the tale he was spinning, so he decided to run with it.

"How the fuck is he yo' new plug? That nigga a narcotics detective, cuz. Unh unh," Gunplay shook his head. "I ain't buying that shit. Yo' ass betta come again."

"That nigga is as crooked as they come, youngin'. He planted a kilo on me and told me if I don't move weight for 'em, then he's gone see to it that I never see the streets again." He informed him. "Our deal is this, he bustes niggaz that's handling and drops the weight off to me for me to move the shit. I'm only seeing twenty percent of the take, on top of that."

When Big Sexy finished telling Gunplay the half truths, he took a breath. It was like he had taken a weight off his shoulders. Now he was waiting to see if Gunplay had bought his story. If he didn't then he knew that was going to be his ass.

"So, you ain't no snitch, cuz?" Gunplay asked, licking his top lip and biting down on his bottom one.

When he said this, Big Sexy's frowned and looked at him with murder bleeding from his eyes. "My nigga, I almost committed suicide right now, 'cause I for damn sho' was 'bouta leap for that gun. Don't chu eva in yo' life mention me and snitching in the same sentence. Hell naw, I'm notta mothafucking snitch!"

Gunplay sighed with relief that he didn't have to kill Big Sexy. He then lowered his gun and lay back in his seat. He took a breath, chest rising to its full potential and then falling.

"Cuz, I almost popped you." Gunplay claimed. "I thought fa sho' you was snitching. Luckily a young nigga decided to ask questions first."

"Yeah, lucky for me, ol' trigga happy ass nigga." Big Sexy cracked a grin, but his heart was thudding crazily. In his head he was thanking God that Gunplay had believed his story.

Gunplay chuckled and scratched his temple with his gun. "Well, at least I know you one hunnit now."

"Check it out though, youngin'," he began. "We gone rock with this narco 'til I figure out how to handle 'em and getta new plug."

"Cool. I'm with that." Gunplay stuck his gun on his hip and pulled his shirt down over it.

"Yo', if it comes down to popping this cat or you down to get the job done?" Big Sexy looked him dead in his eyes. He knew that puffing a cop's wig out could lead to a nigga getting the needle, but he believed that nigga, Gunplay was probably crazy enough to do it.

"Yo,' if it's for the betterment of the team, then I'll get at any nigga, police or not."

Big Sexy grinned and dapped him up, saying, "My nigga."

Afterwards, he fired up the car and pulled out of the alley, heading back into L.A traffic.

When Big Sexy made it to the storage unit and seen all of the kilos he had on his hands, he was smiling from ear to ear and rubbing his hands together greedily. He slapped hands with Gunplay and hugged him, excitedly.

"Yeahhhh, that's what I'm talking about, baby, we back, we back, we back!" Big Sexy slapped hands with the young man and hugged him again. He then picked up the kilo of cocaine he'd uncovered when he broke one of the vases that were stored inside of the van.

Big Sexy already knew that he could get rid of all of the drugs fast. Most of it he was going to get off through wholesale clientele, while the rest he was going to let his street team handle.

"That's what I'm talking about. We 'bouta make it snow out this bitch!" A smiling Gunplay looked at the brick he'd taken from Big Sexy.

Six months later

Malik walked inside of the library. As soon as he crossed the threshold he made his way down the fiction aisle and found the novel he was told to get. After checking the book out, he headed back to his cell. Heading up the stairs and making his way down the tier, he came across one of his homeboys from his hood. They exchanged head nods, communicating to one another that the homeboy would play look out for him while he handled something. Malik made it inside of his cell and opened the book he'd checked out from the library. Halfway through the book there was a rectangle cut out the pages and a cellular phone was embedded inside of it.

The cellular ran Malik five-hundred dollars. That was small paper to him. That little change wouldn't set him back. He made nearly twenty times that trafficking dope in prison. He copped the cell phone from a correctional officer that everybody knew by the name of Mack. Mack had his hands in some of everything illegal in the joint. It was said that he even participated in having a couple of niggaz from warring cars hit. He was as slippery as a barrel of snakes, and not to be trusted, but Malik didn't give a fuck. Homie could get his hands on a jack and he needed one desperately, especially since his shit got snatched when his house had gotten raided a few weeks ago.

Malik looked to his cell's door to make sure there wasn't anyone lurking nearby besides his homeboy. Once he saw that the coast was clear, he removed the cell phone from where it was embedded and powered it on. Afterwards, he dialed the telephone number that he recalled from memory. He pressed the cellular to his ear and walked over to his door. He peered out through the rectangle shaped window. Although his homeboy was watching his back, he still wanted to be extra sure he wouldn't get caught slipping on the jack. The last thing he wanted was to end up in The Hole. Sure he was taking a chance by having a cell phone in his possession in the first place, but the call he was making right this minute could change his life. The man that would hopefully pick up his call could make another call that could have him walking out from behind the walls as a free man.

The telephone rung three times before it was answered.

"Yes?" a man with a deep Spanish Accent picked up.

"Well, damn, my nigga. You been duckin' and dodgin' my mothafuckin' calls and shit. What's up with that?" Malik asked. His brows were wrinkled and he fist was clenching. He was as hot as a fire cracker about old boy avoiding him. He had tried hollering at him several times. He called him from the cell phones of a couple of cats that he knew on lock, and ever time he'd hear his voice he'd hang up on him. Malik tried hitting him up a year ago and he'd changed his number. God was on Malik's side though because one of old boy's hit-men had gotten knocked on a couple of bodies and he shot him his number once he'd hit the pen.

"Who is this?" Old boy asked irritated.

"Mothafucka, you know exactly who it is!" Malik said heatedly. "Now yo' ass got ghost the moment I got hit with the numbers for these bodies, thinkin' I was gone drop a dime on yo' ass, but I didn't. Now I can't say I blame you for distancin' yo' self, but chu coulda at least made sho' a nigga books were straight…all the mothafuckin' business we did."

"I have to go."

"As God as my witness, G, if you hang up on me, I'ma give the Feds enough evidence to crucify yo' ass, Blood. Now, you ain't never known a nigga of my caliber to be no filthy fuckin' rat. I'm as thorough as they come. But you got me fucked up if you think I'ma keep lettin' you play me to the left like some bitch! I'll drop dime on yo' ol' pussy ass, keep thinkin' I'm bluffin'! I ain't got shit to lose besides my rep, but I'm willin' to sacrifice it if it means I get to burn yo' tortilla chip dippin' ass for yo' disloyalty."

There was a moment of silence before the nigga he had called spoke again.

"I'm listening."

"I thought so." Malik responded. He then went on to tell him what was on his mind. "Look, I gotta plan to get my ass up outta here but I'ma need yo' help, and a big bag of money once I'm free."

"Go on…"

Malik went on to discuss all of the details of him breaking out of prison. Once he finally disconnected the call, old boy had agreed to assist him in becoming a free man again.

***

Davino stood under the shade of the tint alongside other patrons who were waiting for their cars as they were being washed. His eyes were focused on his '11 Denali truck which was being waxed by a couple of Mexican men, all of whom looked to be no more than five feet tall.

"Fuck outta here! For real?" Buck said into his cellular as he approached Davino from his left. "Alright then, peace." He disconnected the call and stashed the cell phone inside of his pocket. "Yo,' you ain't gone believe this shit." Buck tapped Davino to garner his attention. The nigga glanced in his direction but turned his focus back on his SUV, watching as it was washed.

"You neva know, give it a shot." Davino said, holding his hands behind his back.

"That nigga Fear is outta the game."

Since Davino came home he'd been taking about expanding his business, but his niggaz had been telling him about how Fear had the streets on lock. He had most of the corners sewn up and wasn't letting anyone eat off of them that wasn't buying from him. Davino, the arrogant and egotistic mothafucka that he was, wanted to go to war with the nigga. The only thing that stopped him was his crew telling him that he didn't have enough money or firepower to beef with him. If it wasn't for that he would have been made it rain bullets on Fear's side of the fence.

Acknowledging that the odds were against him, Davino decided to fall back and got his dollars and his killaz up. His momma didn't raise a fool; he knew if he went to war with Fear he'd have to be well prepared. That was going to be the only way he'd stand a chance against a nigga of his caliber.

Davino frowned up and said, "What chu mean outta the game?"

"He gave up the life. You know his right-hand man, Big Sexy, right?"

"Yeah, who could forget about a nigga with a name as god fucking awful as Big Sexy? I wouldn't be surprised if the man is a dicksucka. Anyway, what's up with 'em?"

"From what I was told, he's the one running the show now." He informed him. "See, Fear was the brains of they whole shit, but he bust his gun too. Fat boy on the other hand was the muscle. He took on the grunt work. He was the head of their hit squad."

"I'm following you."

"From what I understand, Fear is a nigga that there ain't no bargaining with. I'm thinking, maybe his man will be willing to hear us out. I hear he's mo' chill, if you know what I mean."

"Chill?" Davino looked at him for the first time, raising his eyebrow. "That nigga'z a mothafucking head bussa! A straight up killa, like yo' ass. I don't know if chill is in his mothafucking character."

"True that!" Buck nodded in agreement. "But my boy I just finished kicking the bobo with, says the big man will be mo' inclined to listen to reason than his boss. You understand what I'm saying?"

"Hmmm," he massaged his chin as he thought on the situation. "You may have a point. We'll holla at homie first...present 'em with my business proposition. If he doesn't decide to go with it, then we'll make our move. We'll have the element of surprise on our side. Cocksucka will never know what hit 'em."

Davino was confident in making his move against Fear's organization. It had been nearly a year so he had plenty of paper put up and more cap peelaz at his disposal. Now, his crew may have not been as big as Fear's, but they'd made up for their lack of numbers with their ruthlessness. You see, Davino was sure the niggaz on his payroll where willing to take it where most niggaz weren't willing to take it, and that would help him greatly should he decide to bear arms.

"See? Now, that's what I'm talkin' 'bout, dawg. If this nigga don't roll with our program then we gone roll his ass right the fuck over! You feel me?" Buck dapped up Davino. He wore a dead serious expression on his face. He loved getting money, but he loved drama more. In fact, he got off busting his gun and causing mischief.

Man, I hope this fat mothafucka decides to buck so I can rock his big ass to sleep. I got this new thang that's still in the box that a nigga been dying to use, for real!

"Buck, get in contact with that nigga'z peoples and arrange a sit down. Tell 'em to meet in neutral territory." Davino told his enforcer.

"Alright, I'm on it." Buck pulled out his cellular to make a phone call.

Right then, one of the Mexicans that were washing up Davino's truck waved him over with his wash rag. Seeing him, Davino tapped Buck on his arm and motioned for him to follow him. En route, Davino pulled out a knot of dead white men and peeled off two twenty dollar bills. He gave the Mexicans that had been washing his car a Franklin each and took his truck keys. He then hopped in behind the wheel of the SUV and drove off, with Buck finally getting in touch with someone close to Big Sexy.

"Yeah, my people wanna meet somewhere neutral..." Buck said into his cell phone.

CHAPTER FIVE

Big Sexy came through the door of the diner causing the bell residing over it to ring. He looked on either side of him before finding himself a place to sit. As soon as he seated himself, he picked up a menu and opened it. He didn't see anything that was fitting of his appetite so he figured he'd settle on a cup of coffee. Big Sexy sat the menu down and called for the waitress who was on the other side of the diner, taking a shabbily dressed man's order. Seeing that the big man was calling for her attention, she held up one finger for him to give her a moment. She finished jotting down the customer's order, closed the small tablet and took the menu from the patron. After giving the man a smile, she went on about her business which was to see what Big Sexy would like to order. She hadn't even reached his table before he called out to her what he wanted and she was going on about her business. While she was gone, he busied himself by looking out of the large window of the establishment. From his seat he could see everyone pulling up to the spot, which was good for him. When he'd first gotten the call that Davino wanted to chop it up he started to tell him to go fuck himself, but his curiosity had gotten the best of him and he decided to humor his competition's conversation.

Before Big Sexy knew it he was being blinded from over his shoulder by headlights. He looked to the headlights and found that they belonged to a Denali truck. The vehicle parked at the end of the row of vehicles in front of the diner and killed its lights. Looking down the row of parked automobiles, Big Sexy saw two heads inside of the SUV. Instantly, he recognized Davino and his right-hand man, Buck. They abandoned the truck and made their way towards the diner. Seeing them approaching, Big Sexy decided to busy himself with his cell phone, pretending like he wasn't waiting for them to arrive. He didn't even have to look up to see where they were headed. Their auras gave away their presence as they looked around the establishment for Big Sexy. Spotting him, they made their way in his direction.

"Big," Davino addressed Big Sexy when he stopped before him.

Big Sexy slid out from behind the table and said, "Big Sexy."

"Nah, my nigga," Davino shut his eyelids briefly and shook his head. "I'ma grown-ass man, so I'm not finna be callin' anotha grown-ass man Big Sexy. You feel me, dawg?"

"Dully noted."

"Alright then, thanks for takin' this meetin', homie." He shook hands with the giant.

"Don't wet it. I wasn't doin' too mucha shit today, so I thought I'd bless you with my presence for a few ticks." He glanced at his Rolex.

"'Preciate it." He looked back to Buck. "This the Robin to my Batman, Buck."

"'Sup, homeboy?" Big Sexy threw his head back like *What's up?*

"Ain't shit. Look, I'ma let y'all rap for a taste, I'ma fall back." Buck bumped fists with Davino and went on about his business, leaving the two bosses to themselves.

Once Davino had sat down at the table, Big Sexy went on to speak to him. "So, what is it that you wanted to see me about?"

Davino was about to speak, but then the waitress came back with Big Sexy's cup of coffee. She sat it down on the table and went to tend to another patron. Once she had left and Big Sexy had started to fix up his steaming hot cup of dark liquid, Davino decided to go on with the conversation.

"Look, homie, you don't strike me as a bullshit type of nigga, so I'm not gone beat around the bush. I'ma straight shoota with it so I'm just blast from the hip." Davino told him.

Big Sexy nodded as he dumped a small pink bag of sugar inside of his cup of coffee. He then went on to stir the hot beverage up.

"Well, there's no secret that you have most of the Eastside sewn up. I mean, there's hardly any real estate for me and my dogs to eat on." Davino told him. "I do alright with the territory I got on smash, but I could be doing a hell of a lot betta if I had, say, the other side of Adams and Compton Avenue..." he waited to see what Big Sexy was going to say. As soon as he finished what he had in mind, the giant stopped stirring his cup of coffee.

Big Sexy sat his spoon down and pushed aside the saucer that his cup of coffee was sitting on top of. He stared Davino directly in his eyes as he began speaking, "Lemme get chu straight, you want me to give up some of my blocks out of the kindness of my heart, so you and yo' niggaz can eat?"

Davino sat back in his seat and nodded, saying, "The way I see it, those two blocks ain't gone really hurt cho pockets with all of the corners you got. Even if you did lemme hold them cornas down, I'm still not gone be making as much as you would be, but it will appease me."

Big Sexy scowled and responded with, "Nigga, and why in the fuck would I care about appeasing you? As a matter of fact, who in the fuck are you, homie? I don't owe you shit! I mean, yeah, you may have put in some work back in the day, but that ain't saying shit to me! What the fuck are you laying down now? When the last time yo' pistol smoked?"

When Big Sexy said all of this shit, Davino was hotter than an African summer. His eyebrows slanted and he bit down hard on his bottom lip. He clenched his fists tight, causing the veins in his hands to become more pronounced.

"I may not have done no wet work out in these streets in a while, but behind them walls I done soaked up twice as many niggaz as I have out here."

Big Sexy twisted his lips and gave him the side eye, saying, "Again, I'm not impressed. What are you doing right now?"

"I'm gonna be coming across this table and strangle yo' big fat ass in a second." Davino swore, mad dogging the giant with madness dancing in his eyes.

"You come across that table and you gone be sitting yo' ass right back down, homeboy." Big Sexy threatened and sat his handgun down on the table. His eyes locked onto Davino and dared him to make a move. The two gangstas mad dogged each other for what seemed like an eternity. Davino appeared as if he wanted to try the giant. "I see you got it in you. Well, gone and leap, frog! Leap!"

The hostility suddenly left Davino's face and he held his hands up, palms showing. "It's okay, big man. You got that! I don't want no trouble."

"I know you don't want no mothafucking trouble, so roll yo' punk-ass up outta here!" Big Sexy growled lowly.

"I just came here for a sit-down, hoping we could come to some sort of agreement. I guess I was wrong about that. My apologies, Mr. Gangsta." Davino placed his hand to his chest and smiled weakly, trying to hide how pissed off he was. "Have a nice night." He rose from the table and reached for his waistline. Seeing him do this, Big Sexy went to shoot him, feeling that his life was in grave danger. Acknowledging that the giant was about to gun him down, Davino slowed his hand as he brought it towards his waistline. Big Sexy watched carefully as he reached inside of his pocket and pulled out a knot of dead presidents. He peeled off a couple of dollars and dropped them on the table top beside the cup of coffee that Big Sexy had ordered.

"Just thought I'd do the gentlemanly thing and pay for your beverage. You have a nice night," he tipped his fitted cap and turned towards Buck who was sitting at the counter, spitting some G at some fine-ass patron. He whistled sharply in his main man's direction and he turned around on his stool. When Buck did this, Davino saw that he had his cellular out so he figured he was in the middle of programming old girl's telephone number into his contacts. Buck gave his boss a courteous nod before he turned back around on his stool to the young lady he was hollering at. He wrapped up their conversation and bid her a farewell before heading out of the diner's exit. Big Sexy rose from his seat and headed out of the diner behind him. Coming out of the door of the establishment, he made a left out of the door and made his way towards his car which was parked in the front of the diner also. He walked towards his vehicle taking a cautious look over his shoulder. He found Davino stepping off the curb towards the same truck he'd came there in. When he'd opened the driver side door, he looked up in Big Sexy's direction and smiled wickedly.

Big Sexy's eyes widen and his jaw dropped open. That's when he noticed for the first time that Davino's right-hand man, Buck, wasn't anywhere near him. An alarm went off inside of Big Sexy's head. His head snapped to his left and then his right but he didn't see Buck. It wasn't until his eyes had settled on the windshield of his own car that he saw him running up behind him, with a gun pointed at him. Big Sexy ducked down just as the first shot ranged out into the night and cracked a spider's cobweb in the windshield of his vehicle. Hunched down, heart racing and adrenaline pumping, Big Sexy ran to the back of his car with the young gunman licking shots at his ass. While moving, he whipped out his banga, but winded up dropping and kicking it from moving so fast. He knew he was in trouble now, because without his gun he was unable to defend himself. This made him an easy kill for that nigga, Buck.

Buck ran up behind Big Sexy as he made his way around the car. He kicked him in his back and he went crashing face first into the pavement, wincing. He kicked him in his side and made him turn over. He wanted to look him in his eyes before he did away with him, just like he did with all of his victims.

By this time, niggaz and bitchez were scrambling around the parking lot trying to avoid being killed. While some of the patrons inside of the diner faces were glued to the large windows watching everything unfold. It didn't matter to Buck if any of those mothafuckaz saw him pull the trigger because he was masked up.

"That's yo' ass, nigga!" Buck gritted his teeth.

Blowl! Blowl!

Two hot ones to Buck's chest rocked his ass and sent him retreating, holding his chest. He opened fire on the nigga that had popped him as he ran away. The nigga that had popped him was dressed in all black and wearing a blue bandana over the lower half of his face. After taking shots at homie wearing the blue bandana, Buck was running towards Davino's truck as fast as he could. The nigga wearing the blue bandana stopped and lifted his gun. He held it with two hands and opened fire on Buck as he fled.

Blowl! Blowl! Blowl! Blow!

Buck ducked down as the bullets flew over his head and cracked the diner's windows into spider's cobwebs. Having finally made it to Davino's truck, he opened the passenger door and sent some heat at the nigga that was getting at him. His shots punctured holes in nearby vehicles and shattered some of their windows, but no of them manage to hit their intended target. Seeing that he wasn't about to catch up with Buck to finish him off, the gunman wearing the blue bandana over the lower half of his face, stopped chasing after him. He watched as Buck hopped into the front passenger seat of the truck and slammed the door shut as he was driven away. While he was busy observing this, he took the time to eject the magazine out of the bottom of his handgun and smacked in a fresh clip, chambering a copper round into the head of his weapon. Afterwards, he retreated back towards Big Sexy's truck where he found him hunched down beside it. He gave him a signal to let him know that the coast was clear. The big man thanked him before jumping in behind the wheel of his whip and jetting out of the parking lot. Right behind him, there was a Jeep Grand Cherokee toting the gunman that had saved his life and three other killaz.

***

Gunplay and the rest of the killaz sat in the living room watching Big Sexy as he paced the floor. The giant massaged his chin as he thought things over. The dining room was in complete silence as his killaz waited for him to speak his mind. Suddenly, Big Sexy stopped and turned around to his niggaz, clearing his throat with his fist to his mouth.

"Niggaz tried to take my head off tonight," Big Sexy spoke for the first time. "If it wasn't for Gunplay then I'd be lyin' belly up out this bitch. Finished, homie. Y'all niggaz would be mourning me and making funeral arrangements, but by the grace of God, and my young homie's .45 automatic," he placed his hand on Gunplay's shoulder and looked into his eyes, tapping his fist against his chest. He then looked to his killaz again. "I'm still here. A mothafucka is still standing." He took the time to walk around all of his men. "See, that's where that nigga, Davino, and his faggot-ass homeboy fucked up. They shoulda neva missed my big black ass, 'cause now I'ma make 'em pay...with interest."

Big Sexy left the dining room and returned shortly with a small Nike duffle bag. He sat the duffle bag at the center of the dining room table and unzipped it. He then held the bag open for all of the killaz to see. As soon as all of them head busting-ass niggaz seen all of those dead faces, their eyes bugged and their mouths hung open. Some of them even whistled and exchanged glances with whoever was sitting beside them. The sight of that loot got their asses talking among one another. They were talking about all of the shit they could buy if they had that paper in their possession.

"This a nice lil' bag I got here, right?" Big Sexy said, taking in all of the faces of his hittas. They all nodded in agreement. "This like, a hunnit stacks...easy. The nigga I'ma let walk off with this is gone bring me Davino's head."

"Shiiiit, a hunnit stacks? I'd kill that nigga tonight and bring 'em to you." One of the killaz said.

"For a hunnit of them thangs I'd kill myself," another one of the killaz said. He jumped to his feet and drew his gun, pointing it to his temple. This caused everyone to chuckle and laugh. Silence fell on the dining room once that nigga, Big Sexy lifted his bear claw of a hand though.

"The fun and games are ova, my niggaz. If y'all niggaz wanna eat...I mean, eat really good...then deliver me that fool's head, and all this is yours..." he held opened the bag and spared them another look inside at all of the dead presidents. "You know what? Fuck it! Pass this mothafucking bag around my nigga, Gunplay. Let these niggaz see what real money feels like." He passed the duffle bag to the young nigga that had saved his life that night and he went around the table with the bag, letting niggaz pick up stacks and run their thumbs through them. Everybody inside of that room that night was smiling from ear to ear. Niggaz that Big Sexy had never seen crack so much as a fucking grin was smiling like they were told to say 'cheese' before a camera. Once the duffle bag made its way back into Big Sexy's hands, he zipped it back up and slung the strap over his shoulder.

"Remember, bring me that nigga Davino's head…and this bag is yours." Big Sexy patted the duffle bag and then left the room, leaving all of his men talking about how they were going to smoke Davino and get that big ass bag of money.

***

Buck stood up straight as the doctor wrapped his chest with three layers of bandages. Once he was done, he left the killa with a bottle of pain killaz. He was then paid off by Davino and showed the door. As soon as Davino turned around from locking the front door, he found his main-man popping one of the pills and washing it down with a glass of faucet water.

"You good, my nigga?" Davino asked him as he held up the bulletproof Kevlar vest the young gunna had on when he tried to body that nigga, Big Sexy. If it hadn't been for him rocking one that night the homies would have been building him a mural on the block that very same night, but luckily for him he'd thought to wear one out to their meeting.

"I'll be straight just as soon as these pain killaz kick in, dawg." Buck winced.

"Good. Come on," Davino motioned for him to follow him out into the dining room. "It's time I holla at the soldiers."

Davino made his way into the den with Buck bringing up the rear. He found his crew lounging around passing blunts and shooting the shit. Buck stood off to the side of him and he stood tall, taking in the appearance of his clique. Most of the men had been down with him from the beginning, while some of them were fairly new. None of this mattered though. The most important thing to him was that they were all solid and loyal. They would kill and lay down their lives for him, and all he had to do was give the word.

Davino's squad was ignorant to his presence, but once one of them spotted him, he nudged his comrade and alerted him. This set off a domino effect and soon everyone knew that 'boss dawg' was there. Quickly, they straightened up and mashed out the blunts that were in rotation, putting an end to the chattering.

After taking in the presence of every man assembled, Davino went on to tell him about the meeting he'd called with Big Sexy and how it had went left field.

"As of right now, we're at war," Davino said. "I need all of y'all strapped up 24/7 out this bitch. I want y'all hitting all of this bitch-nigga'z corners…every single one of 'em! Kill all them fools, and if you can manage, bring me back that fat nigga'z head. If one of y'all manages to bring me dude's head then I'll set chu out nice. I'll set chu out real nice." He snapped his fingers and motioned Reckless over. The young nigga stepped up with a duffle bag and unzipped it, holding it open for him. Davino reached inside of the bag and started pulling out stack after stack. He stacked the rubber banded money on the table before him, lining them up beside one of another and on top of each other.

"That's a hunnit racks, my niggaz!" Davino announced to his crew. As soon as he said the amount all of their eyes doubled in size and they whistled, whispering among each other right after. "This hunnit racks goes to whoever brings me that mothafucka'z dead body. Straight up! Bring me that man's corpse, and the money is yours!" he swore, looking around at all of the man before him. He could tell by the determined looks on their faces that they were going to try their damndest to bring him Big Sexy's dead body.

***

Duke pulled up inside of the parking lot of The Bar Fly and murdered the engine of his rental. He flipped the sun visor down to look into the rectangle shaped mirror that was there. He looked himself over and confirmed he was looking as debonair as he thought he was when he left his house that night. As of now, he was dressed in an Atlanta Falcons fitted cap and matching sweatshirt. The gold cable chain that hung from around his neck was attached to a miniature tire with a gold Daytona rim. The canary yellow diamonds in his earlobes twinkled as he turned his head from side to side, to get a good look at himself. Having confirmed he was without a doubt one of the fliest niggaz on the scene that night, he hopped out of the car and slammed the door shut behind him.

Duke stuck a toothpick at the corner of his mouth as he made his way across the parking lot, heading for the entrance of the establishment. He pushed the large wooden door of the bar open and was greeted by 2pac's *California Love*. The Bar Fly was dimly lit that night, but it was very much alive with activity. The patrons there were having drinks, smoking, shooting pool and watching T.V on the monitors mounted on all four walls.

Duke strolled inside of the bar, with his gold cable chain rocking back and forth. The lights kissed off of the medallion and the gold Daytona gleamed. He stepped to the bar and sat down on the stool, motioning the bartender over to take his drink order. The bartender, Nigel, held up his finger signaling for him to give him one minute before he tended to him. While waiting on Nigel to attend to him, Duke grabbed a handful of cashews and tossed a couple back. The entire time Duke was keeping a watchful eye on Buck, who was busying with a game of pool.

"What can I get cha, chief?" Nigel asked as he placed his hands down on the bar top. He was a dark skinned man that kept his hair in a short salt & pepper afro. He looked to be around fifty-five or sixty-years-old, but he kept himself in good shape.

"A Corona, pops." Duke glanced at Nigel to give him his order, but he went right back to watching Buck.

"Coming right up," Nigel turned around and grabbed a Corona from where he had it stashed in a cooler of ice cubes, along with several other brands of beer. He then grabbed a bottle-cap opener and popped the top of the Corona he'd retrieved. Discarding the cap, he slid a folded napkin before Duke and sat the Corona down on it.

"Six fifty, black man." Nigel said after presenting him with the beer.

Duke threw back the last of the cashews he was eating and brushed the crumbs from off his hands. He then stood to his feet and pulled out a folded stack of dead faces. He peeled off a twenty dollar bill and dropped it on the bar top.

"Keep the change, pops." Duke picked up the bottle of beer and started in Buck's direction.

"Thanks." Nigel said, picking up the bill.

***

"Alright, 8-ball, right corner pocket," Buck sharpened the head of his pool stick with the blue cube. He then sat the cube on the ledge of the pool table and leaned over it, lining up his shot. He teased the shiny black ball with the tip of his stick, making sure his aim was precise.

"I got two yards that says you won't make that shot." Arty said as he stood on the other side of the pool table. He had two wrinkled one-hundred dollar bills in one hand and a pool stick in the other. His head was shaved on the sides but the top of it was braided into cornrows. He was wearing a white T-shirt and a black leather vest and matching pants. A gold necklace dangled around his neck with a bulldog bust on it. Around his wrist was a spiked leather band.

Buck looked up from where he was about to take the shot from. "Nigga, you ain't saying nothing butta word. Money on the wood makes all bets good." He sung.

"Fa sho'." Arty sat the wrinkled one-hundred dollar bills on the pool table's ledge and sat the beer he was drinking on top of it, pinning it there.

At this time, Duke was playing the background looking like a dark figure sipping on a bottle of beer.

Buck focused his eyes on the 8-ball, teasing it with the head of his pool stick. Once he figured he'd lined the shot up perfectly, he took it. The black ball bounced off the green walls of the pool table top, skinned a striped orange ball and landed into the right corner pocket. As soon as the 8-ball landed into the netted pocket, Arty shut his eyelids and clenched his teeth. He gripped his pool stick so tight that his knuckles turned white. He and Buck were playing $5,000 dollars a game, plus whatever else they betted on the side. So far homie was twenty-one thousand dollar in the hole, but his money was long and he wouldn't stop until he left out of that mothafucka broke.

Buck stood up smiling at Arty and sharpening his pool stick with the blue tube. "You done yet?"

"Fuck naw." Arty claimed. His pride wouldn't let him leave out of The Bar Fly a loser.

"My man," Duke spoke up from the shadows, garnering Arty's attention. He'd just looked up from racking up the pool balls. "I'll buy that game from you."

"You know this nigga, man?" Arty looked at Buck but pointed to Duke.

Buck took a good look at Duke before answering, saying, "Nah, I don't know homie."

Arty finished racking up the balls and stood upright. "Look, homie, we ain't playing for no chump change here. I'm talking 'bout five G-stacks a game. I'm into ya man here real heavy."

"How much?" Duke inquired, taking a sip of his Corona.

Arty looked to Buck smirking, thinking once he told old boy how much he owed he'd get scared and back off, but that wasn't going to happen. "Twenty-one grand."

"That lil' change ain't 'bout nothin'." Duke removed his Presidential Rolex watch and passed it to Arty. "That's forty grand right there, baby. You can keep the change."

A frowning Arty looked over the piece of jewelry. "I don't know jack shit about watches. How I'm 'pose to know this mothafucka is really worth forty stacks?"

"I know jewelry, lemme check it out, Art." Buck took the Rolex from Arty and examined it carefully. Once he was finished he passed the watch back to him.

"Well?" Arty asked, wanting to know if the watch was authentic and worthy of the price tag.

"That mothafucka worth as much as homeboy says it is." He nodded his assurance.

"You've gotcha self a deal." Arty shook Duke's hand. He then snapped his fingers and motioned his wife over. She was dressed in a black leather cap and overalls. Reaching inside of her purse, she removed G-stack after G-stack, stacking them bitches up on the pool table's ledge in front of Buck. "It's all there, you wanna count it?"

"Nah, you good, my nigga," Buck replied to Arty's offer.

"You gentlemen enjoy your night." Arty nodded to Duke and Buck. He then threw his arm over his wife's shoulders and they made their way towards the exit.

"Forty stacks?" Buck frowned. "You must be really eager to play some pool. There's a couple of more tables besides mine you coulda played at and saved yo' self that paypa."

"Yeah. I know, but them other fools don't look like they can play pool. You do."

"Oh, really? Well, what does a nigga that looks like he can play pool look like?"

"Like you."

Buck chuckled and said, "Like me, huh?"

"Yep," Duke replied, sharpening his pool stick with the blue cube.

"My man, what's yo' name, homie?"

"Duke."

They dapped one another up.

"Buck," He exchanged names with him. "Well, Duke, it's five stacks a game. Money on the wood makes all bets good." He smacked a knot of money on the wood grain of the pool table. Right after, Duke was smacking his knot down on top of his knot. With the bets laid down on the table top, they went on to play their game of pool.

Buck and Duke played six games straight. They talked, laughed, and drunk beers on Duke's dime. They seemed to be enjoying one another's company. So much so that you would think the two of them went way back, like a couple of college buddies or some shit.

"Damn, my nigga, you done won four outta the six games." Buck said, racking up the balls inside of the triangle.

"Fuck are you, a professional at this shit?

"Nah, I play a lil' bit." Duke took a swig of his Corona. This was his third beer that night. Once he saw that Buck had finished racking up the balls, he got into position to take his shot. "Say, uh, I gotta confession to make."

"Oh, yeah? What's that?"

"I used this game to get chu comfortable enough for me to ask you what's on my mind." Duke admitted, teasing the Q-ball with head of his pool stick.

Buck's forehead deepened with creases. "Is that, right? Well, I must say. You got my curiosity, so what is it that chu wanna ask me, homeboy?"

"First," Duke began, standing erect and placing his hands on the pool stick. "lemme give you a brief history on me."

Duke went on to tell Buck how he was a get-money-nigga from the other side of the city, who was in dire need of some good cocaine. He also told him how he had heard that him and his man, Davino were the niggaz he needed to see if he wanted to get right.

"My plug fucked around and got knocked, so I'm just out here assed out. I been seeing these fools from around my way for birds, but they shit got too much cut on it and my people ain't tryna fuck with that no mo'. Hell, neither am I for that matter. My reputation was on the line with that bullshit that fool was hittin' me off with."

Buck was silent as he stared at Duke. His eyebrows were arched and his jaws were locked, pulsating. From the expression on Buck's face, Duke could tell that he was mad and annoyed. He didn't give a fuck though. He needed to be in this nigga'z circle if he was going to have things popping in his hood again.

Buck shrugged and responded, "So, what chu telling me all of this shit for? What chu want me to do about it?"

Duke took a deep breath before starting again, "Look, it isn't a secret that your Davino's right-hand man. What I'm askin' is that chu make an introduction for me. Now, don't get me wrong I'm not lookin' for any handouts. I'm willin' to drop a bag on you for pluggin' me in with the Head Honcho."

Buck was pissed off. He felt played. He had really taken a liking to Duke, so to find out that he was looking to get put on just like every other nigga in the city, made him feel like a joke.

"Sorry to disappoint chu, but I don't know any Davino." Buck claimed. He then leaned over the pool table to take his shot.

"Come on now, dawg, everybody knows y'all got the streets on lock. Y'all got the whole pie. I just want a lil' taste is all. You feel me? Help me get in where I fit in and…"

"What, you hard of hearing, my nigga? I said, I don't know no fucking Davino."Buck spat fire as he stood upright. He was .38 hot having discovered that he was being played like a hoe. There wasn't any way in hell he was going to hook Duke's ass up with Davino. As far as he knew, that mothafucka was an undercover cop, and he sure as shit wasn't about to be the reason behind Davino's empire crumbling. Fuck that! Dude would have to find himself another sucker.

"Sixty stacks, right now, in yo' hands, all I want…" the words died in Duke's throat once Buck lifted his shirt and showed him the silver .357 Magnum revolver tucked in his waistline above his belt buckle. The killa'z eyes read murder and his lips were twisted. He looked mad enough to shoot him in there in front of all of those people. Duke was sure he'd do it too; he'd heard plenty of stories about Davino's enforcer. He was definitely not one of those niggaz to play with.

"Fuck all you want, all you gone get is a closed casket, fucking with me." Buck promised. His jaws were clenched so tight that the vein on his forehead threatened to rupture.

Duke looked down at the revolver in Buck's waistline and then back up into his menacing eyes. He mad dogged him and thought about drawing his gun. But he was sure old boy would shoot him down before he was able to clear it from his waistline. With that in mind, Duke sat his pool stick down on the pool table and made his way for the exit. Seeing him leaving, Buck dropped his shirt over his pistol and kicked him in the ass on his way out. Duke stumbled forward and dropped his fitted cap on the floor. He caught himself before he could fall and picked up his fitted cap. Adjusting the cap on his head, he looked around the bar and saw what appeared to be everyone's eyes on him. He was embarrassed, and wanted to get in Buck's ass for playing him in front of everyone, but the heat he'd get for murdering him in front of everyone wasn't worth it. Figuring that it was best to leave the situation alone, he straightened out the wrinkles in his shirt and continued for the exit.

"Bitch-ass nigga, betta keep that shit moving," Buck eyeballed Duke until he'd disappeared through the exit. He then looked across the bar at a couple of guys that were swigging their beers and watching a couple of other niggaz shoot pool. "Any of y'all wanna shoot pool? Five G-stacks a game?"

"I'm straight." One of the guys said.

"Too rich for my blood," another one said, with his hands up in surrender.

"Fuck it! I'll play my damn self." Buck leaned over the pool table to take his shot.

An hour and a half later

A tipsy Buck staggered out of The Bar Fly and made his way over to his car. He'd just stopped before the driver's door of his vehicle and pulled out his keys, when he saw the dude he'd gotten into it with coasting past him. Instantly, he went for the .357 on his waistline. Seeing that he was on his shit, Duke chuckled and smiled at him. He then twiddled his toothpick at the corner of his mouth and tilted his Angels fitted cap at him.

"Bitch-ass nigga," Duke said and sped off down the street.

"Punk-ass nigga don't won't no smoke." Buck spat on the ground and fished his keys out of his pocket. Having found the key that he was looking for, he stuck it into the slot of the lock. As soon as he turned the key the vehicle exploded and sent his black ass flying through the air, missing an arm. The loud explosion set off the alarms of nearby whips. Buck landed face down on the windshield of a parked Nissan Sentra, cracking it into a spider's cobweb. The blood from his face leaked out and outlined the breakage in the glass red. The dead man's eyes were bulged and his mouth was hanging open.

Duke adjusted the side view mirror as he gangsta leaned in his whip. Through the the side view mirror he saw the burning wreckage of the vehicle that Buck had attempted to get into. See, while he was inside of the bar running interference, Gunplay was rigging Buck's car with an explosive set to detonate as soon as he turned the key in the door slot.

"Hahahahahahahahahahaha!" Duke A.k.a Broli laughed manically.

Hearing a car honking at his right, Broli looked through the passenger window and saw Gunplay. The young nigga gave him a nod of acknowledgement and he returned the gesture. Afterwards, the youngsta was speeding off down the street.

With the job done, Broli picked up his cellular and shot Big Sexy a text message to let him know they had completed the mission.

CHAPTER SIX
The next day

A shackled and chained Malik was ushered to a blue van with gates on its windows. His chaperones were two armed corrections officers. After making sure his restraints were secure, the corrections officers opened the door of the van and placed him inside. Before he knew it, both of the officers were in the van and they were driving off. Malik busied himself staring out of the gated windows, watching the scenery change before his eyes. It had been a while since he'd seen the outside, and seeing it now made him realize how precious the smaller things in life were.

Malik knew that he'd never see the outside world as a free man every again. He had himself to thank for that though. You see, the entire trip down to the court house was on the account of him gouging an inmate's eyes out. The punk-ass nigga had witnessed Malik using a contraband cell phone and told prison officials. One of the homies had warned Malik that the cell blocks were going to get raided that day, so he was able to hide the cellular phone in a safe place, but when he found out who had dropped a dime on him, he made it his business to get even. With the deed done, he found himself in the back of the van on his way to court, fighting yet another case.

The transporting van pulled up at a red stop light. The moment it did, a toy monster truck came rolling from off the curb. It drove up to the front wheel of the van, on the driver's side and stopped. The corrections officer behind the wheel forehead creased. He and his partner couldn't help wondering where the toy monster truck had come from. They took in their surroundings, but they couldn't find the operator of the toy in sight. The stop light turned green and the corrections officer made to drive off. Just as he was about to mash on the gas pedal, the toy truck exploded and flipped the van on its side.

The explosion killed the officer behind the wheel, instantly. Flames licked the air and smoke billowed from the toppled van. A moment later, a white van with rusting on it pulled to a stop in front of the wrecked van. Its driver, a man wearing a ski mask and bulletproof vest, sat behind the wheel. While his partner, who was dressed exactly like him, jumped out of the passenger seat. He had an MP-5 in one hand and bolt cutters in the other. Running around the wrecked van, he saw that the corrections officer in the passenger seat was still alive. He was bleeding from his forehead and looked dazed from behind the cracked windshield. Still, the man in the ski mask didn't show him any remorse for his injuries. As he walked past him he pointed his MP-5 at his side of the windshield and pulled the trigger. The automatic weapon spat flames furiously, shattering the windshield and pelting the remaining corrections officer with bullets.

Having killed off the last corrections officer, the man in the ski mask threw the strap of the MP-5 over his shoulder and climbed the top of the van. He removed a tool that was secure in his waistline. This tool was called a 'Slap Hammer'. It was used to pull out a lock's cylinder. He sat the bolt cutters down on the van and injected the Slap Hammer inside of the lock of the van's sliding door. Once the tool had locked in place, he yanked the lock out completely. After he had done this, he removed the lock from his Slap Hammer and slid it back into his waistline. Next, he slid the door of the van open and grabbed Malik's hand. He pulled him out of the van and he stood to his feet. While he was standing upright, the man in the ski mask cut the chains of his shackles and handcuffs. Having had his restraints removed, Malik jumped down from the van. Together, he and the man in the ski mask ran back to the rusting white van. They jumped inside of the van and slammed their doors shut. The ski masked man holding the bolt cutters gave his partner a signal and he drove off in a hurry.

That night

"Yo', man, you think we should take it in now?" Boogie asked Q-Bone, who had just finished serving a crackhead.

"Take it in? Hell naw, we got this mu'fucka jumpin' tonight. It's money out here." Q-Bone told him. "Wait a minute," he folded his arms across his chest and angled his head. "Don't tell me you scared Davino's and nem people gone roll through here, or you?"

It was evident that Boogie was worried from the expression on his face, but he knew better than to admit that, because if he did, his homies would never let him live it down.

The rest of the homeboys started making clucking sounds and walking around, moving their arms like chickens.

"Ol' scary ass nigga!" one of the homies called out.

"Check his drawers, I bet he shit on 'em self." Another homie called out.

"Boog, you shook? Say it ain't so, dawg. Say it ain't so." Another one of the homies said aloud.

"If you scared then go to church." Q-Bone insisted to Boogie.

"Man, mothafuck y'all niggaz," Boogie frowned and waved his homeboys off. "I ain't scared of a goddamn thang. Any niggaz slide up this way," he drew his gun from his waistline and wagged it as he talked. "I'ma wet up his whole shit, for real, for real."

Right then, a late model Regal came to a screeching halt in the middle of the residential block and the back window came down. An AR-15 assault rifle emerged out of the window with an infrared laser. As soon as them mothafuckaz on the block seen it their eyes lit up and their mouths dropped open. Although they had their guns on their waistlines they scrambled away to avoid catching fire. They knew that their pussy ass handguns weren't a match for automatic gunfire.

Blatatatatatatatatatatatat! Buratatatatatatatatat!

Metal jacketed bullets ripped through the air as the barrel of the AR-15 ignited with fire. The firing of the assault rifle flashed light in the darkness of the night. The cherry, which was the red dot laser of the AR, moved from each back of the retreating men, unloading shots in them.

Blatatatat! Buratatatat! Blatatatat! Buratatat! Buratatat! Blatatatat!

The blood curdling screams of men filled the air as they collapsed to the ground, one by one. There wasn't a single soul among the lot that escaped the merciless wrath of the AR-15. They were all cut down with extreme prejudice. When the assault rifle had finished spitting death, its barrel wafted with smoke. The gunman ejected the spent banana clip from out of the rifle and loaded in a new one, chambering a live round inside of its head. The gunman peered out of the back window watching for any movement. Once he clarified that all life had ceased to exist among the group of men he'd laid down, he pulled the AR-15 back inside of the window. Right after, he urged the getaway driver to pull off. The G-ride's tires squealed as he made a hasty getaway from the murder scene.

***

The night was relatively quiet besides the occasional car driving down the block. Every now and then a cool breeze would tickle Rock's neck. This led him to throw his hood over his head and tuck his hands inside of his pockets. He was standing beside a telephone booth on the side of a liquor store, serving dime crack rocks to any crackhead that came looking to cop. The dollars were coming fast and plentiful. His pockets was stuffed full of dead faces, and he was looking to make more before the night was over. Feeling that he was almost done with the work he had on deck, he snuck a peek at what he had left, which was five rocks. Seeing this brought a chipped tooth smile to his face. He took his hands out of his pockets and rubbed them together, trying his best to keep warm in the cool weather.

Hearing his cellular ringing, Rock reached inside of his pocket and looked at the display. Seeing that it was this broad, La'Trece, who he had been trying to bust down for a while now, he smiled and went ahead to answer the call. He had just brought his fist to his mouth and cleared his throat to put on his sexiest voice, when an old ass Lincoln Town Car came to a screeching halt before him. His eyelids stretched wide open and his jaw dropped once he saw a dude emerge halfway out of the window. He wore a black bandana over the lower half of his face and gripped a MAC-10. He pulled the trigger of his rectangle shaped weapon and waved it back and forth across Rock's body. As the machinegun spat rapid fire at Rock, he dropped his cell phone and did a dance on his feet. Twenty holes appeared on his body and his blood went flying everywhere. Once the gunman had finished off the magazine of his MAC-10, he ducked back inside of his G-ride and urged the getaway driver to smash out.

Vroooom!

The Lincoln Town Car sped away as Rock's body hit the sidewalk and bled out. His eyes were bugged and his mouth was stretched open. His cellular lay beside him in his own blood. La' Trece was still on the screen, screaming his name over and over again.

"Rock! Rockk! Rockkkk!"

***

"Y'all niggaz talkin' like y'all shook," Ray Ray said to his homies. He was wearing a beanie and a windbreaker over a white T-shirt. "When they manufactured them niggaz' guns that we warrin' with, they didn't stop makin' the mothafuckaz. Shiiiit, I stay strapped at all times! I wish a nigga would try to creep up on me." He harped up some phlegm and spat on the ground. The moment he did, his entire chest erupted; blood and chunks of flesh sprayed the ground. His homies scattered in every direction not wanting to be the next nigga to get shot. Ray Ray turned around as blood spilled over his chin. His eyes bulged as soon as he saw his ski-mask rocking killa clutching a big ass shotgun. The killa racked the powerful weapon and squeezed off again. The blast sent Ray Ray's beanie flying into the street along with the left side of his face. When he hit the ground you could see half of his bloody skull.

The fool that had blasted Ray Ray stood over his dead body. His eyes were concealed by a pair of black sunglasses. His gloved hands waved his shotgun around looking for some more mothafuckaz to blast on. Unfortunately, all of Ray Ray's homeboys had scattered and gotten too far away for him to dispatch.

At that moment, a Honda skidded to a stop behind him in the middle of the street. Its driver threw open the passenger door and the killa jumped into the seat. He slammed the door shut and pulled himself out of the window, sitting on the door. As the driver drove off down the block, the killa aimed his shotgun at the windows of parked cars and blew them out for the hell of it. The loud roars of the shotgun and exploding window glass could be heard throughout the night.

"Welcome to the Wild Wild West, mothafuckaz! The Wild Wild West!" The killa pointed his shotgun straight up into the air and fire it twice. He then pulled himself back inside of the window as the getaway car continued to speed away.

***

The Yukon raced up the block with its front passenger window slowly descending. It jerked to a stop and a nigga dressed in all black hung halfway out of the window with an AK-47, with a big ass banana clip. He pulled the trigger and the assault rifle rattled to life in his gloved hands. Empty copper shell casings fell from the slot of the weapon as its barrel spat flames. Niggaz were screaming, yelling, and hollering trying to get the fuck out of the way as the AK spat heat. Burgundy blood splattered on the sidewalk as the men fell to their deaths, wearing holes on their backs and chests. Suddenly, the gunman stopped firing and lowered his choppa. He took the time to look over his handiwork. Seeing some of his wounded enemies squirming and groaning, he gave the driver the signal to stay put while he finished them off.

The gunman threw open the door and jumped out of the huge truck. He stepped over the poor bastards that were still unfortunate to have their lives and sprayed them, sending them to meet their Maker. Spotting a man lying on his stomach twitching, he moved to finish him off, stepping in his direction hurriedly. Just when he lifted his assault rifle to hand down his death sentence, something at the corner of his eye garnered his attention. His head snapped in its direction. At the end of his line of vision he saw one of the men he'd shot. He was bleeding at the shoulder and mad dogging him, pointing a gun right at him. For a minute they stood where they were trying to decide what should come next, and then it happened, homeboy on the ground opened fire.

Bloc! Bloc! Bloc!

The gunman took three to the chest and swung his AK around. One last shot to his forehead snapped his head back and sent his brain spraying out the back of his skull. He fell over dead, lying on his back over another dead man's body. The driver's eyes bulged and his jaw dropped open. He threw his truck in *drive* and floored the pedal. The SUV squealed as it sped off. Homeboy on the ground followed the truck with his gun, blazing shots at it as it sped off.

Bloc! Bloc! Bloc! Bloc!

Bullets ripped through the back of the Yukon as it continued to speed down the block with the front
passenger door hanging open.

***

Buuuzzzzzzz!

The hair-clippers made a loud buzzing sound as it handled the task that it was specifically crafted for. Malik stood before the men's room mirror with his eyelids narrowed into slits, shaving off his thick bush of hair. It fell in follicles and bunches to the floor, littering the surrounding areas of his bare feet. Once he was done, he sat the hair-clippers down on the sink. He then brushed the loose hairs from off his neck, his ears and chest, with the palm of his hand. Afterwards, he looked himself over in the mirror, turning his head from side to side. He knew that this would undoubtedly be his last time seeing his handsome face. As much as he didn't want to go through with the procedure, it had to be done in order for him to move around without having to worrying about the authorities taking him in. Having been broken out of prison, he was a wanted man now and his face was on every news channel and news paper in the country. There wouldn't be a badge in the United States that didn't know what he looked like. And knowing the police at that day and age, they'd be trigger happy and couldn't wait to put something piping hot in his ass.

"Mr. Simpson are you ready?" a feminine voice came from the other side of the door.

He took a deep breath and his shoulders slumped, still holding his gaze in the mirror. "Yeah, I'm ready." He responded and slipped on his hospital gown, tying it at the end of his back. After giving himself one last look in his reflection, he made his way out of the bathroom.

Malik was placed on a gurney and rolled into surgery. An oxygen mask was placed over his nose and mouth. He was then gassed with a sedative until he eventually fell asleep. As soon as he was out, the surgeon got right to work giving him a new look. By the time he awakened he'd be a new man...a brand new man.

***

A few days after the surgery, Malik found himself sitting up in bed watching T.V. His face and head were wrapped in bandages. As soon as he saw the doctor that had performed his plastic surgery entered his room, he picked up the remote control and turned off the television. He'd been dying to see what he looked like under the bandages and couldn't wait to get them off. The doctor approached the bed and handed Malik a handheld mirror. He then removed the small metal piece that held the bandages in place on his face. He sat the piece down on the rolling table and begun unwrapping his patient. Malik's heart was thudding, and with each layer of bandage that was removed the harder his heart thudded. In fact, the only things he could hear at that time were the beating of his heart, as he focused his eyes on his reflection in the handheld mirror.

The doctor finished unwrapping Malik's face and stepped away, allowing his patient to get a good look at himself. Malik's eyes were as wide as saucers and his mouth was hanging open. He was touching his face like it didn't belong to him...like it wasn't his face...like it was someone else's face.

"I...I look just like him now," Malik stated the obvious, still touching his face. It was still a little swollen from the procedure, but in a few more days his appearance would be back to normal.

"Like who?" the doctor frowned and asked.

"Fear," Malik didn't answer.

***

Malik stood in the mirror of the men's rest room again, looking himself over. He was dressed in a black Nike cap and matching tracksuit. Hearing a knock at the door, he kept his eyes on his reflection and told the knocker to enter. The door came open and one of the men that Gustavo had sent to bust Malik out of prison was standing there. He was holding a small duffle bag and his face was solemn. He was dressed in a plaid shirt and brown leather cowboy boots. Malik took the small duffle bag from the man and he left the rest room, pulling the door shut behind him. Malik then sat the duffle bag in the sink and unzipped it. He found several bankrolls of Benjamin Franklins with rubber bands tangled around them. He smiled when he seen all of that money. Next, he unzipped the compartment at the end of the bag. Opening it, he found a passport, social security card, driver's license, etc. He placed these items back inside of the bag and zipped it back up. This time, he unzipped the opposite end of the bag. Once he reached inside of the compartment, he pulled out a Glock 50. and two fully loaded magazines. Malik checked the magazine that was already inside of the handgun and smacked it back in. He then chambered a bullet inside of the gun and tucked it at the front of his pants. Right then, he heard his cellular ringing and vibrating.

Malik inspected the duffle bag until he found the cellular on the side of it in a compartment. He unzipped it and reached inside, feeling the ringing cell phone in his hand. He brought the cell up to his face and looked at its screen. There was a telephone number there he wasn't familiar with. Curious as to who was calling the device, he pressed answer and placed it to his ear.

"What's brackin'?" Malik said into the cell phone.

"I take it you have everything you demanded now." Gustavo stated.

"Yeah, everything except the car."

"It's waiting for you outside. It's a charcoal gray 2006 Chevy Impala. The keys are on the back tire, on the driver's side."

"Good lookin' out." Malik hoisted the strap of the duffle bag over his shoulder.

"Now that you have all that you've requested. I trust that you'll keep your mouth shut."

"Word is bond." He responded, looking into the mirror and touching his face. He turned his face from left to right, acting like one of those niggaz in the Gillette commercials after shaving.

Gustavo disconnected the call and Malik stuck the cellular phone into his tracksuit's pocket. He then opened the rest room's door and made his way out.

***

The sun was beaming down on Malik, projecting its rainbows. He looked up at it and held his hand above his brows, frowning as he stared up at it. Having seen enough, Malik looked ahead and saw a '06 Chevy Impala sitting on stock rims, parked across the street. Malik jogged out of the parking lot and across the street. He snatched the keys from where Gustavo said they'd be located. He then opened the driver's door and tossed his duffle bag into the passenger seat. Right after, he stuck the key into the ignition and turned it. The vehicle instantly started up. Once he'd put the automobile in drive, he looked into the side view mirror and pulled off.

***

Big Sexy had just poured himself a drink when he heard a knock at the door. He screwed the cap back on the bottle of dark liquor and sat it back down on the counter, and pulled out his gun. Having seen who it was through the peephole, he relaxed and tucked his gun on his waistline. Next, he opened his door and stepped aside so his guest could enter.

"Homie, what the fuck is going on?" Broli asked as he was let inside of the house.

"What chu mean?" Big Sexy's forehead creased.

Broli snatched the toothpick from out of his mouth and said, "These streets are on fiyah, G. All them bodies out there," he pointed over his shoulder with his toothpick. "Is bad for business, bruh, real bad for business."

"Man, fuck that! Niggaz try to take my head, so I answered back. Can't have mothafuckaz out here thinking I'm sweet." Big Sexy answered back heatedly. "If that pussy-ass nigga Davino take one of mine then I'ma make it my business to take two of his, ya dig?"

"I feel you on that," he sat down on the arm of the couch, twiddling the toothpick at the corner of his mouth. "But if these bodies keep falling then my people are gone be out looking for answers and niggaz to pin bodies on. And if that happens, then they gone start applying pressure on niggaz and then mothafuckaz are gone end up talking. Then you know what I gotta do, big man? I gotta take care of any nigga out here that knows a lil' mo' about me than necessary," With that having been said, he gave Big Sexy a knowing look. This let the giant know that he meant he'd have to kill him for fear that he may drop a dime on him. He already knew he was willing to snitch should he found himself backed into a corner, so he couldn't gamble prison time on him. Fuck that!

"Check this out, dawg. I feel where you coming from, but those bitch-ass niggaz started this shit." Big Sexy told him. "If I fallback now, then fools gone think my people soft, and I can't have that."

Broli nodded and massaged his chin, thinking about everything that Big Sexy had said to him. He raised some pretty valid points, but still, if the bodies kept dropping then they were going to catch heat of epic proportions. Having come to a conclusion, Broli let his hand down to his side and looked up at Big Sexy.

"I'll tell you what, lemme take care of this Davino character." He told him. "I'll see to it that he's outta your hair forever, you feel me?"

"As tempting as that offer sounds, I'm gonna have to decline it." Big Sexy responded. "You see this exceeds business. It ceased to be that once that cocksucka took a shot at me. When that first shot rang out, it made this shit personal."

Frustrated, Broli blew hard and ran his hand down his face. It seemed as if Big Sexy wasn't trying to hear what he was saying. He figured that the giant's mind was made up, so he may as well stop trying to make him see things his way.

"Alright, fuck it," Broli rose from the arm of the couch with his hands up in surrender. He was letting Big Sexy know that he was done with the situation. "You want him then you got 'em, but if my people get involved, don't come calling me. 'Cause the only nigga'z ass I'm looking to save is this nigga standing before you right now. If I was you, I'd start looking for a couple of fall-guys that don't know too mucha shit. That'll be the only way you'll be able to get cho self outta the shit-hole you currently digging from murdering all of these niggaz out here."

"I'll keep that in mind." Big Sexy replied.

"You had better." He dapped him up and made his departure.

CHAPTER SEVEN

Reckless sat behind the wheel of his burgundy '03 Honda station wagon. His head was on a swivel as his gun with the extended magazine lay in his lap. He had to keep a close eye out on things as he waited for his boss to return. They were currently at war with Big Sexy and his crew, so the murder rate in South Central Los Angeles had rocketed, largely due to them.

Hearing a car approaching from down the street, Reckless adjusted his side view mirror and peered into it. He saw a black on black Mazda coming up fast. Instantly, his adrenaline began pumping with a vengeance and his heart was beating out of control. He gripped his gun tight while focusing his attention on the side view mirror. He was almost positive that whoever was approaching was the opposition. And once they stopped near his vehicle, he was going to make them regret picking the wrong side in the drug war.

Reckless was about to hang out of the window and give the Mazda hell, but the automobile raced right past him. The sounds of Biggie Smalls' *Mo' Money Mo' Problems* thumped furiously from its speakers. The racing car bent a left at the corner, barely stopping a second at the stop sign.

Reckless took a breath and slumped in his seat. He thanked God that he hadn't started busting on the approaching car. It was one thang to kill a mothafucka that his crew was beefing with, but to take an innocent life would definitely weigh on his conscience. He wasn't like most of those niggaz out there; he actually cared if he killed an innocent bystander.

Reckless lifted his O's fitted cap from off his crown and scratched his head. He'd just smacked the cap back on his head when he saw Davino coming out of Buck's baby's momma's house. The look in his eyes held great sadness and he could tell he was on the verge of crying. Seeing his homeboy like this fucked with Reckless's emotions. For as long as he'd known the gangsta he'd never shown anything less than strength and confidence, but now that had changed. He figured losing someone as close to you as Buck was to him could do that to a man, because it had definitely done it to him. The only difference was Reckless was doing a better job than Davino holding it together.

Davino opened the passenger door and hopped into the front seat. He then slammed the door shut behind him and slid down in his seat. He didn't say a word to Reckless as he stared through the windshield at nothing in particular.

"Damn," Davino shook his head and shut his eyelids, tears streamed down his cheeks. "I can't believe they got my nigga Buck, man. That was my mothafucking heart right there, G." He pounded his fist to his chest. He licked his lips and bowed his head, more tears dripping.

Reckless looked at Davino and felt his pain. Buck had taught Reckless everything he knew about killing. In fact, he'd caught his first body with him. He was the first nigga to put a gun in his hands, and on top of that, he gave him a hustle so he could eat. Before him he was wandering through the streets homeless, snatching purses and eating out of fucking garbage cans. The young nigga was sleeping on bus stops and park benches. But when Buck came along, he changed his circumstances. He was like God to him, he performed a miracle. He took a bum-ass nigga from the streets and turned him into something.

It was safe to say Reckless loved Buck like a brotha. And the mothafuckaz responsible for his death were going to regret the day they ever decided to lay hands on it.

"I feel yo' pain. Buck was my mothafuckin' nigga too." Reckless assured him.

"It's all good though. I got them young boys that's eager to prove themselves to shoot up that fat mothafucka'z grand momma's house." Davino told him.

"Is that right?"

"Yep." He nodded.

That night

A Crown Victoria pulled up alongside the curb of a residential block. Its driver killed its headlight, but left the vehicle idling. He then slid down in the seat and spoke to the two men in the backseat. He told them to hop out and handle their business while he waited for them.

"...Spray that old ass bitch house up and get the fuck back to the car." The driver told them on a very serious tip. He then checked the magazine of his handgun and smacked it back into the bottom of it, chambering round into its head.

"Alright, come on, B-Rat," one of the men in the backseat told his homeboy. They were both masked up and had just finished locking and loading their Uzis.

Together, the young boys that Davino were referring to, hop out of the Crown Victoria. They shut their respective doors shut quietly and jogged across the street, keeping a close eye on things. They hopped over the gate of the house before them, made their way up the driveway and hopped the fence into the backyard. They came out on the other side of another house where they'd ended up in its front yard. After coming out of that yard, they stood out in the middle of the residential street, in front of a large white two story house. They nodded to one another and lifted their Uzis. Pointing their automatic weapons, they pulled the triggers and they rattled to life. Fire flickered from the muzzles of the Uzis and tatted up the house, blowing what looked like one million holes through the front of the house. Splinters flew from the white wood of the house and dust and rocks flew from the concrete steps. Once the young boys had finished firing, they ejected the magazines from their weapons and reloaded them. They gave the house another quick spray before retreating back in the direction where'd they'd just came from.

As soon as the young boys made it back to the Crown Victoria, the driver threw it into drive and pulled off from the scene in a hurry, leaving smoke from the vehicle's exhaust pipes in its wake.

***

"...Alright, I love you, too." Big Sexy disconnected the call and mashed out what was left of the cigarette he'd been smoking during the conversation.

Big Sexy had just gotten off the phone with his grandmother. She'd informed him that her house had been shot up. Luckily for her she wasn't at home, she was at Bingo at the time. Needless to say, granny was in fear for her life and devastated at what had happened to her home. Although Big Sexy had promised to buy her a brand new house in a better neighborhood, she wasn't trying to hear him. She'd been living in the house for over thirty-five years and she'd be damned if she moved now. Realizing that his grandmother wasn't going to move out of the house, Big Sexy told her he'd pay for the damages and made arrangements for her to stay at a hotel.

"Mothafuckaz wanna go after families and shit? Dick suckas wanna play with me? Okay then. We can play. I got toys to play with." Big Sexy flipped over the couch and tore open the bottom of it. Reaching inside, he pulled out a chrome shotgun. He then picked his handgun up from the coffee table. He held the weapons up at his shoulders, looking between them and smiling evilly.

Big Sexy lowered the guns at his sides and marched back inside of his bedroom. He tossed the weapons upon the bed and got dressed in black clothing. He then pulled a black beanie over his head and tucked a black bandana into his back pocket. Next, he slipped on his gloves and stashed his weapons inside of a long duffle bag. He then grabbed the duffle bag up and walked towards the front door. He'd just unlocked the door and pulled it open when a thought came to mind.

Fuck am I doing? I don't even know where this nigga is at! I'ma fuck around and get popped with these straps rolling around in the streets, aimlessly. Up in here running off on emotions when I needa be smart and calculated, Big Sexy thought to himself. He shut the door and locked it back, running his hand down his face. He walked over to the other couch and sat down, sitting the long duffle bag down between his legs. Leaning forward, he steepled his hands underneath his chin and gazed aimlessly. *Fuck it! I'ma have to holla at this nigga, Broli and let 'em work his magic.*

Big Sexy pulled out his cellular and flipped it open, making a call to Broli.

"Yo', I needa holla at chu about something, my nigg." Big Sexy said into his cellular as soon as Broli picked up his phone.

An hour later

Big Sexy sat before the large window at Denny's restaurant picking over the scrambled eggs of his Grand Slam. He wasn't in the slightest bit interested in the meal; he'd just ordered it so he'd blend in with the rest of the scarce patrons of the establishment. He was actually there waiting on Broli to arrive. Big Sexy found himself looking at his watch for the seventeenth time in the past half hour.

111

Tranay Adams

Frustrated, he shook his head and pulled out his cellular. He was about to hit that nigga, Broli up to see what the fuck was taking him so long.

"Where the fuck is this nigga, man? Got me up here waiting and shit." Broli flipped open his cell phone and searched his contacts for the name he had in mind. He was about to make the call until he saw someone pulling up into the parking lot at the corner of his eye. Looking over his shoulder, he saw a new model Charger. It had pitch black tinted windows and chrome rims that gleamed under the little light that illuminated from the restaurant's window. The driver's door opened and Broli stepped out. He slammed the door shut behind him. He then went on to adjust his Braves fitted cap and his leather jacket. The crooked law enforcer didn't seem to notice Big Sexy as he made his way towards the double door entrance of Denny's. As he walked towards his destination, the giant got glimpses of the holstered Glock on his waistline.

"It's about fucking time, man. Fucking cops think they own the world." Big Sexy picked up his Berry Blend drink and took a sip. He then sat it back down when he saw a waitress showing Broli to his booth. She had planned on seating him at a booth on the furthest side of the restaurant, but Broli insisted on sitting down at the booth directly behind Big Sexy. As soon as he sat down he was given a menu which he quickly looked over before ordering a Grand Slam himself. Only thing he didn't get was a Berry Blend juice. He opted for a cup of black coffee.

"Will that be all?" the spunky, blonde haired waitress inquired.

"Yeah, thanks." Broli handed her his menu and she went on about her business. She returned shortly with his cup of coffee. It wasn't until then that he finally decided to address Big Sexy. "So, to what do I owe the pleasure of this meeting?"

"First off, where the fuck have you been? I've been up at this bitch a lil' over an hour," Big Sexy told him. He had a hint of anger in his voice, but inside he was fuming. He hated when mothafuckaz had him waiting or bullshitted around. The way he saw it, that wasted time could have been spent handling business.

"My bad, big man," he replied and then took a sip of coffee. "I had some pussy on the line I've been tryna get for the past four months, I hadda get it. I couldn't let that fine mothafucka get by me. You know how it is."

"Unfortunately I don't, it's money over pussy with me."

"Anyway, nigga, what the fuck you won't?"

"You know that nuisance you offered to take care of for me?"

"Who we talking about here…Davino?"

"Bingo."

Hearing that Big Sexy wanted him to put the love on Davino caused Broli to smile. His scandalous ass loved doing dirt, especially since he knew that he practically had a License to Kill.

"Soooo, what brought on this sudden change of heart?"Broli asked.

Big Sexy was about to answer Broli's question, but then the waitress arrived with his meal. Once she'd left, the giant went on with what he had to say.

"Well, I was gone pop the nigga myself, but I figure why not let chu do it? That way I can keep the heat off me."

"My nigga," Broli said, laughing like Denzel. "Now you thinking with the big head and not the small head. That's what I'm talking about. Work smarter not harder, big man. Don't worry about nothing either, I'ma take care of this nigga for you. Once he's gone, this lil' war will be over."

"How you figure, nigga?" Big Sexy's forehead crinkled.

"Kill the head and the body will follow."

Big Sexy nodded in agreement and then said, "Check this out though. I wanna be there when you do the job."

"And why the fuck is that? I thought a smart man would wanna be as far away from a murder as possible."

"True, true, true," He nodded. "But I want that mothafucka to know I beat 'em before he shuts his eyes forever. You feel me?"

"I got chu. Now get the fuck from outta here so I can enjoy my meal in peace."

With that having been said, Big Sexy slid out from behind his table and pulled out a knot of dead presidents. He peeled off a crispy fifty dollar bill and dropped it on the table top. Afterwards, he made to leave but Broli called him back. When he turned around, Broli pointed to his food, signaling for him to pay for his meal. Big Sexy blew hard and walked over to Broli's table. He pulled out his money again and dropped another bill on the table top, pinning it down with a Hunts ketchup bottle.

"Thanks, big man." Broli said. He then went to work on his Grand Slam.

***

It was two o'clock in the morning when Broli came by Big Sexy's house to pick him up. They stopped at McDonald's and grabbed a couple of sausage McMuffin combo meals, before heading out to their destination. They ate their food along the way and even chopped it up about your everyday bullshit. After a while they quieted down and listened to the radio. By this time, Big Sexy had fallen asleep and the sun was on the creep.

Broli made a left turn into a recreational center and drove deep inside of it. He coasted past the sandbox, the swings, the jungle gym, the rest room and the gymnasium. At this time it was dawn, and Broli was getting closer to the destination. In fact, he saw the nigga he had left chained up to a tree and nudged Big Sexy until he awoke. Big Sexy awoke yawning and stretched his arms. He licked his ashy lips and wiped the scum that had accumulated at the corners of his eyes with his knuckles. Right after, he sat up in the passenger seat and looked around.

"What's up, man? Where this nigga at?" Big Sexy inquired, looking over at Broli.

"He's chained to that tree ahead." Broli nodded to Davino.

Broli pulled up about twenty feet away from the tree he'd chained Davino to. From where he was sitting inside of the car, Big Sexy could tell that Davino was naked. He appeared to be slumped too, head bowed so you could see the top of his scalp. Big Sexy couldn't help wondering what Broli's wicked ass had done to him. Knowing how the crooked law dog got down, he knew that it wasn't anything less than demonic.

Broli killed the engine of his BMW and looked out of his window at Davino. He was smiling at him when he slid a fresh toothpick at the corner of his mouth. He kept his eyes on him as he pulled out a pair of black leather gloves and slid them onto his hands, flexing his fingers in them.

"Yes, sir, there our lil' friend is. I told you I'd deliver." Broli looked to Big Sexy. "Did I, big man?"

"Yes. You did." Big Sexy nodded. He had to admit that he was impressed with the time it had taken Broli to find Davino's ass and have him at their mercy. This made him happy he'd called him to handle the job instead of riding around aimlessly looking for him.

"Do me a favor, homeboy. Pop that glove-box and hand me that banga that's in there." Broli nodded to the glove-box. Big Sexy pulled his hand inside of the sleeve of his hoodie and used his hand to open the glove-box. When he opened the glove-box he found a .45 automatic handgun with a silencer on its barrel. Using his hand he'd covered with his sleeve, he picked up the handgun and passed it to Broli. Broli accepted the handgun and checked its magazine. Seeing that it was fully loaded, he smacked the magazine back into the butt of the weapon and chambered a hollow tip round into its head. "Alright, let's go say hello."

Broli threw open the door and hopped out of his car. Once Big Sexy had come from the opposite side of the vehicle and stood beside him, they started for the tree that Davino was chained to naked. The closer they got to Davino the more his wounds became more pronounced to Big Sexy. He was bloody and covered in bites he'd more than likely suffered from squirrels and whatever else was gnawing on his black ass since he'd been left chained to a tree overnight.

A broken beehive lay at Davino's feet. The sound of buzzing filled the air. It looked like one-thousand bees were circling him. Davino swung his head from left to right as the bees swarmed his head, stinging him mercilessly. He hollered out in pain and thrashed against the chain that restrained him against the tree. He desperately tried to swat the annoying bees away but his hands couldn't reach his head.

Ahhhh, fuck! Fuck, man! God—goddamn it!" Davino threw his head back cursing. His face had swollen badly due to him being allergic to bee stings. "Ah! Ah! Ah! Sh— shit! Dammit!"

"Hahahahahahahaha!" Broli laughed as he and Big Sexy approached Davino.

Hearing Broli's terrifying laughter, Davino forgot about the tyranny of the angry bees. His head snapped up and he looked from Big Sexy to Broli. As soon as he saw them his heart thudded and his stomach dropped. His bladder grew hot and he assumed he was going to piss on himself, but nothing manifested.

"Big Sexy, man, lemme go and I'll call off my hittas. We'll fallback and leave the game to you, my nigga! I don't won't nothing, them lil' punk-ass cornas will be yours." Davino pleaded, sounding like a straight up bitch. His hardcore gangsta image had faded, and all that was left was the bitch that lurked in him the entire time.

"Oh, now you wanna fallback and leave things be, huh? Nah, homie! Shit don't work that way. You see, you came at the king and missed. So now you gotta answer for that. Duces!" Big Sexy threw up two fingers and headed back towards the car. As he trekked back to the vehicle he could hear Davino screaming aloud for him to spare his life. Big Sexy didn't bother to turn around to witness his enemy's execution. The muffled sounds of Broli's gun firing were enough to confirm his death for him.

By the time Big Sexy had hopped back into the passenger seat and slammed the door shut, Broli was tossing the murder weapon on the ground and making his way back to his car. Walking towards his vehicle, he pulled off his black leather gloves and jumped in behind the wheel. Afterwards, he tossed the gloves inside of the glove-box and smacked it shut. He fired up his BMW and pulled away from the killing field.

"You see how that shit got handled, big dawg?" Broli looked back and forth between the windshield and Broli. "I found the nigga that was giving you problems, and then I took care of his ass. He's gone now, finito."

"Good looking out, my nigga." Big Sexy stated his appreciation.

"Nah, ain't no good looking out. I'm just taking care of business." Broil told him. "Anybody standing in the way of our progress gots ta go. They gots ta get eliminated. You feel me?" he took his hand away from the steering wheel and held his fist out to Big Sexy.

"Fa sho'." He dapped him up.

"We gotta beautiful arrangement here, my nigga, so let's not fuck it up." Broli told him as he drove through the streets. "I supply you with the weight, you get it off, and everybody gets paid. On top of that, if you run into any beef, I can eliminate the opposition, just like I eliminated that bitch-ass nigga back there."

"Much respect." Big Sexy nodded, tapping his fist to chest.

CHAPTER EIGHT
2012/Three nights later

Fear came out of the trees of the mountain top. He had a line with several fish he'd caught himself and a spear down at his side. He smiled from ear to ear when he saw Hahn who was sweeping the porch. He held up the fish he'd caught and his master smiled at him, giving him a nod of approval. Just then, the smile disappeared from Hahn's face and he looked beyond his pupil. Coming out of the trees he saw a big bear sniffing around. The beast's eyes landed on the fish that Fear had in his possession. Wondering what had caught his teacher's eyes, Fear glanced over his shoulder. When he saw the bear, his eyes bugged and the saliva in his mouth dried. He swallowed the lump of nervousness in his throat and gripped his spear tight, causing his knuckles to bulge.

Fear threw the line with the fish on it up towards a nearby tree. The hook of the line landed around one of the tree's branches.

"I'm going to get the rifle!" Hahn called out to Fear and then he ran back inside of the cabin.

The bear looked to the fish Fear had thrown up into the tree and then to him. He was pissed off that the fish were too high up for him to get. The animal's blackened claw extended out of its paws and it stood up on its hind legs, roaring loudly. The beast's large wet tongue and sharp teeth were on full display. Seeing that the bear was in attack mode, Fear took his spear into both hands and mad dogged the bear. He then roared as loud as he could at it. Lowering his head, his nostrils flared and he clenched his teeth, causing his jaws to pulsate.

The bear went charging at Fear and he went charging at it. As they were about to collide, Fear cocked his stick back and swung it against the animal's head. The wooden spear broke in half and splinters went flying everywhere. The bear came back down on its legs and rubbed the side of its head, whimpering. Seeing that he'd hurt the animal, Fear searched the ground for the other half of his broken spear. Finding it, he picked it up, approaching the beast. He did fancy martial arts moves with the sticks, as he and the bear circled one another.

"Raaaooorrrrrrr!" the bear roared loudly.

"Raaaooorrrrrrr!" Fear roared back at him.

Hahn, who Fear didn't know ran inside of the cabin, ran back outside with the assault rifle trying desperately to load in its clip. While he was busy with the sniper rifle, Fear and the bear charged one another again. The bear took several swipes at Fear, but he moved lightening fast dodging the ferocious animal's razor sharp claws. Fear's training with the weights on his ankles and the stones in his backpack over time had him moving super swiftly. The bear couldn't touch him no matter how hard he tried.

Snikt!

The bear roared and took another swipe at Fear, tearing off the lower half of his shirt. Fear looked down at his ruined shirt and seemingly got angrier. Right after, he was attacking the bear heatedly. He beat the beast's head and shoulder's like a pair of drums, drawing wails of pain from it. He continued to strike the hostile bear upside its head and shoulders, until it eventually smacked both halves of the spear from his hands. Seeing that the animal was in close quarters of him and could seriously harm or kill him, Fear did back flips away from it. Once he stopped, he was a great distance away from the bear and had plenty of fighting room.

Fear ran over to some rocks he saw scattered not too far from one another on the ground. Kneeling down, he started grabbing them and launching them in the bear's direction. The first one struck the bear in its head and caused it to holler out in pain. The second one struck the bridge of its nose while the others struck him in the forehead and temple. This further angered the bear and made him dizzy. It shook off his dizzy spell and went charging after Fear who took off running towards the cabin. In motion, Fear looked ahead to see Hahn locking a jacketed round inside of the sniper rifle. Seeing his pupil in danger, he tossed it up into the air at him.

Fear slid across the ground like he was trying to reach home base. Keeping his eyes on the rifle as he slid in the dirt, he lifted his hands to catch the high caliber weapon. Grasping it, he swung around to the animal as he was sliding in the dirt. The bear leaped into the air and Fear aimed upwards at it, looking through the scope of the sniper rifle. With one eyelid closed, he rested his finger on the trigger and waiting until the beast's chest lined up with the crosshairs of his rifle. Once it did, he pulled the trigger and fire spat from his weapon.

Choot!

The bear fell to the ground hard. Lying on its stomach, it crawled after Fear hastily, trying to slash his legs with his powerful claws. Fear backed up in a hurry, repositioning his rifle so he could take another shot at it. Seeing the angry animal cock back its huge paw, Fear flipped over on his stomach and pointed his rifle at it. He squeezed the trigger and the rifle shook, as it spat fire and spilled empty shell casings. The sharp missile shaped bullets took the beast's skull apart and blew his brains all over the fucking place. The bear dropped dead on the spot and Fear sighed with relief, relieving the trigger of the rifle.

Right then, Hahn came walking up. His shadow eclipsed Fear as he lay on the ground. He looked up at his master as he extended his hand downward. Fear got upon his bending knees and grasped Hahn's hand, letting him pull him to his feet.

"Are you, okay?" Hahn asked.

"Yeah, I'm straight." Fear nodded. He then brushed the dirt from off his shirt and shorts. "What're we gonna do with him?" he asked of the bear he'd killed.

"Well, the cabin could use a good floor rug."

Fear chuckled and patted Hahn on his shoulder. "Come on."

Fear threw the strap of his rifle over his shoulder. He and Hahn then walked towards the slain bear.

Hahn went on to teach Fear any and everything he needed to know about the art of murder. After confronting death in the lynching, Fear's bravery had been solidified. He passed that little test with easily. With that out of the way, Hahn went on to show Fear how to calm himself when critically wounded to slow his heart rate and blood flow so that he wouldn't bleed to death. Next, he demonstrated, with a knife, the points of the human body to attack to kill a man quick and proficiently. He also showed him the proper way to yield the knife and use it as a weapon. Once Hahn was sure that Fear had devoured his lessons, he moved him on to guns.

***

Glass bottles lined the log that lay on the ground. Fear watched attentively as Hahn placed the last empty glass bottle down on the log. He then pulled a handgun from off his waistline and screwed a silencer on the end of its barrel.

"This," Hahn held up the handgun with the silencer. "Is one of the most powerful weapons in the world."

Fear's forehead wrinkled and he scratched his temple, saying, "What's the other?"

"Your dick, Alvin Son, do you know why? Because your dick gives life and your gun can take it." He answered his own question. "Today's lesson is about guns. Guns, guns, guns."

Hahn gave Fear the handgun he'd screwed the silencer on. He then stepped behind him. His face was masked with seriousness as he informed his student on how to properly hold a firearm. Fear was holding the gun sideways, so he had to show him the right way. "There you go. See now, the way you see them fools holding their guns in those hood movies is all wrong. You won't hit jack shit that way, but like this, this way not only the proper way to hold your weapon, but it also increases your chances of hitting your mark." Once Hahn was sure that his pupil had his aimed locked, he went onto give further instructions. "Okay now. Spread your legs apart." He told Fear and he obliged. "Alright, I'ma step away now."

Hahn stepped from behind Fear and went to stand off to the side. He looked from his pupil to the glass bottle he was aiming at on the log. There was a moment of silence as she was making sure her sighting was lined up with her target. Then the explosions came.

Shatter!

Fear hit his first target and went on down the line to finish off the rest of them.

Shatter! Shatter! Shatter! Shatter!

The empty bottles exploded as bullets went through them, green glass and clear glass rained down to the ground. Fear lowered his smoking handgun and cracking a smile. He looked to Hahn who folded his arms across his chest and smiled, nodding his approval.

***

Fear practiced shooting the bottles a couple of more times. He then went on to practicing shooting moving targets. From there Hahn showed them how to kill someone up close.

"When executing a mark, it's always best to get 'em from afar, but if it's necessary to get close, then you wanna get just close enough." Hahn told him. "Not too close though. You see, you don't want his blood and/or hair follicles clinging to your clothing. Believe me when I say that forensics are a pain in the ass, you don't want your mistake to come back to haunt chu. Okay," he pointed his handgun with the silencer on its barrel at a dummy hanging from the same tree that he'd hung Fear from. The adult sized doll had a plastic head and a cotton, stuffed cloth body. The body had a diagram of the human beings, mostly vital organs which were located on the left side. If any of these organs were to be severely damaged, death would be the result.

"Once you're close enough, give 'em one to the head," he pointed the gun at the dummy's head. "When he falls, stand back and give 'em two to the sternum to finish 'em off. You got that?" Fear, who had a concentrated and determined look on his face nodded. "Good. Now, you try."

Hahn flipped the gun over in his hand so that the barrel would be in his hand and outstretched it towards Fear.

Later that day

Fear lay on his stomach beneath the shade of a tree. Hahn peered down below with an expensive pair of sleek, black, electronic binoculars. He worked the buttons and knob on the side of binoculars and the front of it extended. Neon blue lights flashed on and off around its lenses. A green light stayed lit at the center of the binoculars and its antenna stood tall.

"Alright, there that cocksucka is. Just in time for his funeral." Hahn sat the binoculars down and picked his silenced sniper rifle up from its opened case. He slid on the last attachments and chambered a missile shape jacketed bullet into the assault rifle. Having made sure the deadly weapon was prepared, Hahn passed it to Fear, telling him how to hold and fire it. Fear took the sniper rifle and rested his eye against the scope. His face wrinkled with his concentration. "Alright now, line it up with either his chest or his head, whichever you please." He looked from the scope to the sighting of the rifle, trying to see if Fear was following his instructions. Through the scope there was a slim, white dude with tattoos over his face and arms. He was wearing a fishermen's hat and attire. He had a fishing pole in one hand and a line in the other. At that moment, he was heading back up to his cabin which was on the opposite mountain top. The line held several fish he'd caught. "You got it?"

"Yep, right on his chest."

"Excellent. Now watch his chest as it slowly rises and falls with each beat of his heart," Hahn coached him. "Watch closely, because I want you to become one with the beating of his heart. Fall in sync with it, become one with it. You are it and it is you." He fell back for a few moments, allowing Fear to merge with the beat of the man's heart. Once he felt like they had become one, he continued with his coaching of him. "Now, very gently place your finger on the trigger, don't pull it just yet. Wait until that moment."

"What moment exactly?"

"*That* moment," Hahn replied. "I can't describe it, but you'll feel it when it comes. It'll let chu know when it's time to squeeze the trigger."

Choot!

The white dude dropped instantly.

Fear lowered the scope of the rifle from his eye, smiling. Hahn, who was very proud of him, patted him on his shoulder and commended him on a job well done.

"You executed him beautifully." Hahn told him. "Now let's get the shovels and stuff so we can bury him, and see about collecting our earnings."

Fear switched hands with the sniper rifle and got to his feet, brushing the dirt from off his jeans. He then disassembled the rifle and placed it back inside of its casing. He shut the case, locked it and picked it up by its handle. Together, he and his master got the shovels and a bag of industrial strength lye so that they could bury their kill.

***

Once Fear and Hahn reached their kill, Hahn checked him to make sure he was the man that he'd been contracted to murder. The only way he had to identify him was through his tattoos. The photo that had been texted to his burnout cellular was of a younger man with hardly any ink. See, this may come as a surprise, but once Hahn found out he was dying, he got back into the murder for hire game. He planned on leaving his goddaughter and her daughter with as much money as he could so they wouldn't have any worries financially. He'd gotten the call to dispatch that poor son of a bitch at his feet the day before. It just so happened that he'd spotted him chopping logs for fire wood a couple of days ago. He couldn't believe the coincidence, but he was glad he'd be able to make some easy money.

The white dude that Fear had killed off went by the name, Hitt-Man. He was a white supremacist hitta behind the wall that told on some very powerful people within his organization to guarantee his freedom. Once he was released he had a bounty on his head so he fled out to the mountains to escape street persecution. Unfortunately for him, he picked the very same mountains that one of the most dangerous men in the world had chosen to train his protégé.

"Yeah, this is him. Let's get to work." Hahn told Fear and took his shovel into both hands.

"Okay." Fear gripped his shovel with both hands and began digging.

Fear and Hahn dug a six feet deep hole. They threw Hitt-Man inside of the hole and covered his body completely in lye. They then shoveled the dirt upon him. Once they were finished, they rehydrated with canteens of water and made their way up to their kill's cabin. They cleaned the place so that there wasn't any sign of his presence there and then they left.

***

Fear and Hahn made their way down from Hitt-Man's cabin, tired and dirty. Having finished up the job he was hired for, Hahn pulled out his burnout cellular and sent a text to his employer, letting him know that the contract had been fulfilled.

Afterwards, he stashed the cell phone in his pocket.

"I'll give you your cut outta the money you paid me for your training."

"Nah, you good. With the skills you teaching me, I'll be able to make that paper back and then some."

"Are you for certain?" he cracked a grin and threw his arm over his shoulders.

"Yeah, you leave that money to yo' family, we good."

"Thank you."

"Nah, thank you."

***

Hahn left the living room and came back with a haggard, thick, cherry brown book with a unique design engraved on its cover. The cover had a human skull with snakes coming out of its eye sockets and swords forming an X behind it. There were rusted gold hinges at both ends of it and a rusted latch with a pad lock attached. The book had information about killing that dated way back to the 1800s, during the medieval era, until present day.

Every killa that the book had been passed to placed new information inside of it, including its latest owner. Its information was priceless to an assassin. Hahn took a necklace from around his neck that was held a golden skeleton key. He used the key to unlock the pad-lock and flipped the latch open. He then opened the book and turned it to Fear. On the first beige, tattered page was a long list of rules dating back centuries ago.

"These are the rules of L.O.E," Hahn started. "You will learn them for they are your gospel. And you shall adhere to them like they are the words of your Lord and Savior. Do you follow me?" Fear nodded, looking over the set of rules as his master went on. "Excellent," he nodded. "The penalties for breaking said rules are as follows." He slid a finger down the lines of penalties for breaking the codes aligning the page. Fear's eyes scrolled down the raggedy page. The punishments for violations ranged from whip lashings, to beatings, to executions. "No one is above L.O.E, not even me." Hahn said. "You must follow the rules. If you violate them you will face the underlying punishments. Got that?"

"Fa sho'," Fear nodded.

"As part of your training, you will learn this book from cover to cover, just as I did." Hahn closed the book and set it on the table top. He then looped the necklace that held the skeleton key around Fear's neck and patted him on his shoulder. Right after, he left the living room and returned with a white towel and a Zippo lighter. Coming back inside of the kitchen, pulled open the cupboard above the stove. Reaching inside, he took down a bottle of Jack Daniel's. He then walked back over to Fear and pulled out a chair for him to sit down.

Having sat down, Hahn laid the towel over his leg. He then passed Fear the bottle of Jack Daniel's and opened up the lighter with a flick of his wrist. "Go ahead and drink it. It's best to get a nice buzz going before I proceed with this." he told Fear.

Fear looked from the Jack bottle to Hahn, forehead creasing. "What's all of this?"

"I'm gonna singe off the tips of your fingers and toes. Should you ever wind up in police custody, you'll be harder to identify."

"That's smart."

Fear twisted the cap off the Jack Daniel's bottle and took it to the head. His throat rolled up and down his neck as he guzzled the strong dark liquor. He brought the bottle down and wiped his lips with the back of his hand. Afterwards, he took the bottle to the head again until he felt himself becoming tipsy. Next, he placed his hand on the towel and lifted his fingers.

A flame sprung from the lighter once Hahn struck the round metal ball in a downward motion. He held Fear's fingers while he went about the task of burning off the tips of them. Fear grimaced and squared his jaws, feeling the bluish yellow flame licking up his finger tip. His foot tapped the floor slowly at first, but then it sped up the longer he felt the hot flame.

"Gaaa!" Fear's face balled up and he squared his jaws, vein bulging at his temple.

***

Hahn put A & D ointment on Fear's fingertips and toe tips. He then wrapped them in band-aids. Fear was as good as drunk now, which was fine by Hahn because he still wasn't done with him yet. After he snapped his Zippo lighter shut and snatched the blood splotched towel from his leg, he stored the items away and disappeared into the master bedroom. He returned shortly with a leather bag and sat it on the table top. Opening it, he began removing all of the tools and items he'd need to give someone a tattoo. Once he was done, he sat down in the chair he'd been in previously and placed Fear's hand on the table top. After preparing his tattoo-gun with ink, he cleaned Fear's hand with alcohol and started on the tattoo. When Hahn had finished, Fear had L.O. E inked on the side of his hand.

Fear looked at his tattoo smiling, drunkenly. He then laid his hand beside Hahn's tattooed hand. Both of the men wore the same ink. The only differences in the tattoos were Fear's was obviously fresher, while Hahn's was fading.

"What exactly does L.O.E stand for?" Fear questioned.

"Loyalty Over Everything, or League of Executioners," Hahn answered as he applied ointment to Fear's tattoo which his skin had swollen around.

"How many of y'all was it when you first started?"

"Including me? Five in total," He held up five fingers.

"Oh, yeah? What happened to them?" Fear asked, looking at his tattoo.

Hahn took a deep breath before answering Fear's question. "Gustavo had all of them killed. They joined forces to help me fight against his people, but they were all eventually murdered. That's when I went into hiding and found a new profession."

"Damn, I'm sorry for your loss." He looked upon him with sympathetic eyes.

"So, am I." Hahn said regretfully. He hated that he allowed his comrades to join him in his crusade against

Gustavo. Had he kept them out of his personal affairs they may have all been alive today. "Go ahead and get started reading the book tonight. I'm gonna go ahead and hit the sack. Goodnight, Alvin Son." He patted him on his shoulder and journeyed back inside of his bedroom, coughing along the way. Suddenly, his legs buckled and he fell against the wall, barely holding himself up.

"Master Hahn," Fear rose from his chair to go to help him. He took three steps before Hahn was lifting his hand, signaling for him to stop.

"I'll be just fine, son. Go ahead and start on your book." He pulled a handkerchief from out of garbs and held it to him mouth. He coughed into it as he headed towards his bedroom. Once he was inside of his bedroom, he shut the door.

Sitting back down at the table, Fear picked up the book that Hahn had given him. He started reading it, but hearing his master coughing as violently as he was stopped him. He wanted to go to his aid, but he knew he'd only turn him away. With that in mind, Fear went on to read the sacred book.

For the rest of Fear's stay up in the cabin, he studied the book. The book had information on the human anatomy, the human psyche, war tactics and strategies, amongst several other things.

***

Hahn faced Fear as they stood in the lake. His hand was on the top of Fear's head while the other was holding his arm. Today was the day that he was going to be baptized. His ceremony was taking place for him to be reborn...as a professional hit-man.

Hahn gave a sermon that ended with, "Alvin Son, I hereby baptize you in unholy water," he dunked his student into the water, quickly pulling him back up.

Fear was soaked and beads of water were running down his face, dripping from off his chin.

Excited about having graduated to another level of the game, Fear hugged his master affectionately. Taken off guard by the sudden act of endearment, Hahn reluctantly hugged the youngsta back. He smiled proudly as he looked down at his pupil. Although he'd trained him to be the best at a very ugly trade, he was still impressed at how he'd taken to things. The art of murder seemed to be second nature to him. It was as if he was born to do the shit, and all he needed was the right guidance to recognize his gift.

That night

"I can tell y'all right now what these niggaz thinkin'." Reckless said as he stood before the last of Davino's foot soldiers. He took the time to take a pull from his burning blunt and blow out a cloud of smoke. He'd called a meeting at his girlfriend's house as soon as he heard about what happened to Davino. He told the soldiers about it and they were hot. They all had mad love for Davino. Not only did homeboy pay well, he often kicked in a few extra dollars to them on the love. "They thinkin' 'cause Davino and Buck are dead that our blocks are up for the takin', but I say they got us fucked up! What they don't know is they ain't takin' shit of ours! I got the plug in pocket so our corners are still gonna be rockin'! All we gotta do is lay these niggaz down, lay low for a while and get back to gettin' this money!" He walked over to the kitchen table in the crack house and mashed out what was left of the blunt. Next, he picked up an AK-47 and chambered a copper missile shaped jacketed bullet into its head. Turning to the collective, he continued to address them. "Now, I can go after these niggaz myself, on some one man army type of shit, but I'm sure I'll be cut down before I take out the lot of 'em. So, I need y'all help. I need y'all to arm y'all selves and ride with me. Ride with me so we can get our corners back and ensure that niggaz eat." He looked around at all of the faces gathered. All of them were twisted into hateful, vengeful expressions. "So, what's up y'all? Is y'all niggaz ready to ride with me and hold shit down, to guarantee that our families eat?"

"Yeah!" the collective said in unison. The men were either holding handguns or automatic weapons, which they held up in the air.

"That's what I'm talkin' 'bout y'all, now here's the plan..." Reckless went on to tell his niggaz the strategy he planned on using in carrying out the executions of Big Sexy and his soldiers.

Food 4 Less parking lot

Big Sexy was leant against the side of his vehicle with his hands in the pockets of his jacket, waiting for Gunplay to arrive. It was 7:30 P.M, and he'd been there since 7 o'clock, the meeting time that he and Gunplay agreed upon. The giant found himself glancing at his Rolex occasionally, wondering why his young homie hadn't pulled up yet. Having gotten tired of waiting, Big Sexy turned around and opened the driver's door of his car. He was about to slid into the driver's seat when he heard someone driving up. Turning around, he saw a royal blue '96 Chevrolet Impala. The hood classic pulled into the parking space, two stalls over from Big Sexy's vehicle. Kurupt's *Girl's All Pause*, which had the automobile's trunk rattling, died as soon as the man behind the wheel murdered its engine.

Gunplay hopped out of his Chevy and slammed the door shut as he started in Big Sexy's direction. Reaching him, he dapped him up and gave him a gangsta hug.

"So, what's up, Big? What chu wanted me to do for you?" Gunplay asked as he rubbed his hands together. He wasn't cold or nothing. He rubbed his hands together like this out of habit.

"I gotta move I need you to make. You my number two so you the only one I trust to do this shit. And you can't tell anyone about this shit either, ya dig?"

"You dug, big homie."

"Good." Big Sexy ducked inside of his car and grabbed the package he had for Gunplay off the passenger seat. He then passed it to him. "Oh, and this is the address." He then reached inside of his back pocket and pulled out a folded piece of paper, passing it to Gunplay as well.

"Who am I 'pose to be giving this to? And what the hell is it, anyway?"

Big Sexy folded his arms across his chest and took a breath, saying, "That package is for Broli. I want chu to make sure he gets it."

"Look, Big, you know I'm not the type to be dipping all in a 'notha nigga'z business, but since I'm making this drop, I needa know what's this is about."

"It's about me getting out from under this nigga'z clutches."

Big Sexy chopped it up with Gunplay a while longer, before he found himself looking at his watch again.

"Yo,' I'ma get up witchu later. I needa get up outta here."

"Alright. And don't worry about nothing, cuz. I got chu faded." Gunplay dapped him up and retreated back to his car.

As Gunplay was starting up his whip and pulling out of his parking space, Big Sexy's cellular was ringing. He pulled it out of his pocket and held it to his ear as he pulled the door of his vehicle open.

"Who is this?" Big Sexy said into the cellular, slamming the door shut behind him.

"This Reckless."

"Reckless? Davino's people?"

"Yep."

For a minute there was silence. Big Sexy didn't know what to say. He was expecting Reckless to start talking big shit, threatening to kill him and shit, but he hadn't. At that moment, he wondered what kind of time the young nigga was on so he decided to play it cool.

"'Sup, nigga?"

"Look, man, I'm willing to let bygones be bygones." Reckless started. "I'd like to leave the past in the past and move forward. You know what I'm saying?"

"I feel you." Big Sexy switched hands with his cell phone. He then fired up his ride and backed out of the parking space, pulling off. "But what kind of guarantee do I have that you and yours ain't gone kick some more shit up, besides y'all laying face up in a coffin?"

"You don't." he admitted. "I don't expect you to take my word for it, either. But look at it like this. With the big homies being gone, I don't have anyone to keep hitting me off with work so me and my niggaz can eat. You on the other hand do. I figure if we make peace then maybe we can talk numbers, you feel me?"

"Most def'," Big Sexy nodded.

"I'd like to give you a lil' peace offering. You know, so you know I ain't bullshitting here, and that I'm dead ass serious."

"When?"

"Shit, tonight if you up to it."

"Yeah, I'm up to it. Gemme an address." Big Sexy pulled the car over and parked. He popped open the glove-box and grabbed an ink pen and a napkin from out of it. Holding the cell phone to his ear with his shoulder, he held the napkin to the car's horn and jotted down the address he had requested. Once he'd done this, he looked the address over and nodded his head. "Alright, homie, I got chu. See you in an hour." He disconnected the call.

***

Reckless disconnected the call and looked up at the soldiers, rolling his AK-47 up in a blanket. He then slid his cell phone into his pocket and addressed the soldiers, "Alright, I got this sucka, ducka-ass nigga to agree to meet up with me. When he shows up, we gone slaughter his big ass…we gone do this shit for Davino."

"Yeah, Davino." One of the soldiers spoke aloud.

"Okay then. Let's go see this bitch-ass nigga." Reckless motioned for the soldiers to follow him as he headed for the door.

The few of the soldiers that still had their guns out, tucked them shits on their waistlines and fell in step behind Reckless, walking towards the front door.

Italia pushed open the glass door of Planet Fitness as she crossed the threshold. She made her way through the parking lot, zipping up her jacket and adjusting her purse strap on her shoulder. Seeing her vehicle in her sights, she pulled out her car keys and unlocked the car. The locks popped and she made her way around to the driver's door. She pulled open the door and jumped in behind the wheel, sitting her purse on the front passenger seat. She had just stuck her key into the ignition when she locked eyes with a pair of menacing ones in the backseat.

"Fear?" Italia gasped her lover's name. Her eyes bugged and her mouth dropped open. Although it was her fiancé in the backseat, she could feel that there was something off about him. She found her heart thudding and stomach turning.

Italia went to throw open the door and run, but he snatched her back inside of the car by her hair. Italia kicked and tried to pry his gloved hand from her hair, but her efforts were useless. Her assailant held a folded rag over her mouth. Instantly, she smelled an intoxicant on the rag which had began to suffocate her. Her nostrils burned and her vision became blurry. She fought on desperately, but her movements began to slow. It was then that she found herself coming in and out of consciousness. Her eyes rolled to the back of her head, and finally, she slumped in her seat.

***

Verna, Fear's mother, came pushing her shopping cart out of the supermarket. She made her way across the parking lot, walking past an automobile that was pulling out of its space. Having made it to her car, she popped the trunk and started putting shopping bags inside of it. Unbeknownst to her, in the back of her, a man wearing a hood and a bandana over the lower half of his face was pretending to rifle through the trunk of his vehicle for something. But what he really was doing was dousing a rag with a substance from a small brown bottle. Once he was done with the bottle, he screwed the top on it and stuck it inside of the pocket of his hoodie. He then looked up and down the parking lot. Seeing that there weren't any witnesses in sight, he crept up behind Verna and suffocated her with the rag. Verna reacted the same way Italia had when she came into contact with the intoxicant. Before she knew it, she was going limp in her assailant's arms and he was dragging her back towards the trunk of his vehicle. He duct taped her wrists and ankles. Next, he dropped the roll of duct tape inside of the trunk and slammed it shut. Afterwards, he straightened out his clothing, and looked up and down the parking lot to see if anyone was around to have seen him. Confirming that there wasn't anyone around, he walked around to the driver's door of his whip and pulled it open. Jumping in behind the wheel, he cranked up his ride and pulled out of the parking space.

CHAPTER NINE

Fear had finally completed his training and it was time to go home. He and Hahn packed up their stuff and made their way down the stone steps. They loaded their bags into the trunk of Hahn's Buick and climbed inside of the vehicle. As soon as Hahn pulled off, Fear powered on his cellular and hit his people up. The first person he called was Italia. The entire time her phone was ringing he was smiling from ear to ear. Hahn looked over at Fear and smiled. He knew that smile on a man's face too well. It was a smile only a special woman could give a man. It was a smile of love.

Italia's phone rang and rang until her voice mail picked up the call. As soon as the recording finished, Fear left her a message.

"Hey, lover, guess who's on their way home. I'll see you in a couple of hours. I love you." Fear said into the cellular and then disconnected the call.

As soon as Fear hung up, he got a text message from Big Sexy that erased the smile from off his face.

By the time u read this u will have finished your training. Congrats! I'm gonna need you to put those new skills to use. I got a situation. Meet me here at 9 tonight…

Big Sexy went on to give him the address of the location. Fear memorized the address and turned his cell face down in his lap. He then massaged his chin as he stared out of the window, watching the scenery change before his eyes.

Hahn looked back and forth between him and the windshield, brows wrinkled. "What concerns you, Alvin Son?"

"My homeboy, Sex, has a situation back home," he informed him. "I gotta bring out the guns."

"So soon, huh?"

"Yeah, but that's my nigga, I'ma always bust my guns for 'em, you Griff me?"

"I got chu...loyalty over everything."

"That's right."

Having said that, Fear let his seat back and shut his eyelids. He knew he'd be back into the thick of the streets once he reached the city again, so he wanted to get as much rest as possible so he'd be prepared for what lay ahead.

***

Hahn pulled his Buick up in front of Fear's house and put the car into park, allowing it to idle. He then nudged his pupil awake. Fear winced as he opened his eyelids. He yawned and stretched his arms. Afterwards, he put the seat up in its proper position. Turning around, he dapped up Hahn and thanked him for training him. He then hopped out of the car and made his way around to the rear of it. As soon as he heard Hahn pop the trunk open, he lifted it and recovered his duffle bag. He started towards his house, but hearing Hahn honk his horn at him, he turned around. The old man motioned for him to come back to his car and he obliged him, coming to the driver's window.

"Take these," Hahn handed his a cell phone, a copper key and a folded note.

"What's all of this for?" Fear's forehead creased.

"The key is to my home out in Paramount. The address is written on that piece of paper." Hahn told him. "Down the basement there's a secret door. Search for the hollow sounding space on the wall, knock on it like this..." he knocked on his vehicle's dashboard in a special rhythmic pattern.

"Inside you'll find every weapon and disguise I used while I was in the game. They are all yours now."

"Thanks, Master Hahn." Fear said. He then held up the cellular phone he'd given him. "And this?"

"I got all of my jobs through that cell. It never stops ringing." He informed him. "Keep in mind, son. The day you answer that phone and take a contract, there's no turning back. You'll be walking through a door that you can't walk back through. You understand?"

"Yes, Master Hahn."

"Good." Hahn replied and put his car into drive, indicating to Fear that he was about to drive off.

"Text me your goddaughter's home address. I'm gonna come by to check on you from time to time."

"Will do."

Fear walked away from the car, but it never pulled off. Suddenly, the driver's door of the Buick swung open and Hahn stepped out. He turned in Fear's direction, seeing his back as he walked away from him.

"Alvin Son," Hahn called out to him. When Fear turned around, he found his master with his arms open. "I'd like a proper goodbye."

In that moment, Fear dropped his duffle bag at his feet and sped walked over to Hahn. He hugged him like a father would his son. When Hahn tried to break their embrace, Fear held fast to him, not wanting to let him go. Acknowledging this, Hahn grinned and continued hugging him.

"I'll see you soon." Fear told Hahn, teary eyed.

The old man nodded and jumped back behind the wheel of his Buick. He threw his vehicle into *drive* and pulled off.

With a heavy heart, Fear slung the strap of his duffle bag over his shoulder and trekked back towards his house. The tears that were in his eyes eventually slid down his cheeks. His weeping was due to Master Hahn pending death. He could tell by his physical appearance and his diminishing heath that he didn't have much longer to live.

He loved the old man like a second father. He taught him so much about life and other things. Just like his biological father had. When he was finally laid to rest he knew that another part of him would die that he could never get back.

Fear unlocked the door of his house and crossed the threshold. Shutting the door behind him, he took a good look at his place. Everything was how he'd left it, and it was clean. It also smelled of Vanilla incents. He owed his thanks to Italia. Not only could the girl cook. She cleaned, ran his bath water, ironed his clothes, supported his dreams and fulfilled his needs sexually.

Thinking of how he had a damn good woman by his side brought a smile to Fear's face. Before he knew it, he had crossed the living room and picked up the portrait of him and Italia sitting on the mantle above the fireplace. Seeing her face caused him to smile further. He couldn't help thinking of how blessed he was to have her in his life. She was his one and only. His ride or die. His everything.

"I love you, lil' mama," Fear kissed Italia's face on the portrait. He then sat it back down where he'd gotten it and headed to his bedroom. Dropping his duffle bag at the foot of his bed, he undressed and took a shower. Once he hopped out, he snatched the towel from off the rack and dried off. He threw on his underwear and opened his closet. He took a gun case down from the top shelf of the closet where he had it hidden behind some books and among other stuff. He sat the gun case down on his bed and popped its locks. When he opened it, there was an Uzi and three magazines and a box of ammo.

Having made sure his Uzi was still there, Fear headed back inside of the closet. He pushed the clothes that were hanging on the rack aside and revealed a sheathed katana. He picked up the katana and searched the clothes. Finding his duster, he grabbed it by the hanger it was hanging on and brought it out of the closet. He threw the duster on the bed and stepped before his dresser's mirror. Holding up the katana, he drew it from its sheath and the light kissed off its blade. The sharp, shiny metal gleamed blindingly.

Fear tossed the sheath upon the dresser and positioned himself, holding up the katana. Right then, he practiced swinging the deadly blade like he had been trained to do.

"Yeah, this definitely not what niggaz want!" Fear said of his skills with the katana. He knew with all of his training that he'd be a force to be reckoned with.

***

Gustavo was shiny from sweat as he ran on the inclined treadmill, huffing and puffing. He had earphones in his ears and he cellular was attached to a Velcro strap-on around his arm. Occasionally, he'd snatch the white towel from off the handlebars of the treadmill and wipe his face and chest off. He'd then place it back on the handlebars and keep running. Hearing his cell phone ringing, he took it off the Velcro strap-on around his arm and looked at the display. Seeing who it was, he programmed the treadmill to be vertical and slowed it down. Walking briskly, he answered the incoming call.

"Mr. Cryler, I hope you have some good news for me," He spoke aloud, continuing his walk on the treadmill.

"I wasn't able to locate Hahn, it's like the guy fell off the face of the planet. However, I was success in tracking down his goddaughter and her daughter." The P.I reported.

"Well, that's exceptional news." Gustavo smirked. He knew that by finding someone related to Hahn he'd eventually find him.

"I'm glad you're pleased, Mr. El Rey."

"Bring whatever information you have on her tonight."

"You got it. I'll be over just as soon as I drop my daughter off at her mother's house."

"Good. See you then."

Gustavo disconnected the call and placed his cell phone back on his arm. A smile stretched across his face as returned the treadmill back to its original settings and continued his exercising.

I'm coming for you, you black bastard. Full speed ahead!

***

Big Sexy pulled to the back of the warehouse where he'd been told by Reckless to meet him. He looked around but he didn't see anyone. His brows furrowed and he picked up his cellular, flipping it open. He redialed the number that Reckless had hit him up from earlier that night. Reckless picked up on the second ring.

"'Sup wit it?" Reckless said into the cell phone.

"'Sup? Yo,' where you at? I'm here." Big Sexy told him.

"For real? I'm here. Nigga, where you at? I don't see you."

Big Sexy looked ahead through his windshield and then through his back window. His brows furrowed further and he said, "I don't see you out here, man."

"It is pretty dark out here. Flash yo' headlight for me, homie."

Big Sexy did as he was instructed. As soon as the headlights flashed, Reckless appeared on the driver side of his vehicle with his AK-47. Seeing something out of the corner of his eye, Big Sexy turned around to see his crafty ass. Reckless smiled wickedly behind his ski mask and pulled the trigger of his assault rifle. The automatic weapon vibrated in his gloved hands as it spat fire, empty shell casings dancing on the ground. When Reckless let up off the trigger of his AK, his eyes bulged and his mouth dropped open. His firing on Big Sexy's automobile had only left scratches behind.

At that moment, Big Sexy came out of the sunroof of his vehicle gripping an AK-47 and laughing his ass off. He knocked on the windshield of his vehicle and said, "Bulletproof, mothafucka!" he then scowled at Reckless and started busting at his ass. His automatic weapon shook in his hands as it spat flames at his enemy. Reckless ducked and ran. He dove to the ground, tucking and rolling like a ball of hay. While in motion, he pulled out a grenade and sprung to his feet, swinging his AK around and spitting heat at Big Sexy. While this was going on, Big Sexy was reloading his AK-47. His was quite a distance away and Reckless's aim wasn't accurate, so he missed. Reckless's bullets deflected off Big Sexy's automobile.

"Bulletproof, huh? Well, how about grenade-proof, dicksucka!" Reckless snatched the ring out of his grenade and rolled it towards Big Sexy's car. Seeing the grenade rolling towards him, Big Sexy hurriedly climbed out of the sunroof of his vehicle. Kneeling down on the rooftop of his vehicle, he leaped just as the grenade stopped underneath his car. Right as he leaped, the impact from the explosion lifted his car off its tires and landed it on its rooftop.

Big Sexy hit the ground hard and grimaced, still holding tight to his AK-47. Lying where he was on the ground, he looked up trying his best to see through the smoke and flames. Through narrowed eyelids he saw Reckless making calculated steps towards him, his AK aimed at him. The son of a bitch was smiling as wickedly as he was before, feeling like he had the giant at his mercy, which he did. Big Sexy, still wincing, looked down at his leg. He could tell from the painful sensation in his ankle that it had been sprung from the fall.

Reckless stopped where he was, standing over Big Sexy with his AK pointed down at him.

"This is for Davino!" Reckless's terrifying eyes bored down at his enemy as he clenched his teeth, flexing the muscles in his jaws.

Reckless was about to pull the trigger of his AK when he was suddenly blinded by the headlights of several automobiles. A group of vehicles swarmed into the location. Reckless knew that these weren't the cars of his homeboys so that meant they had to belong to Big Sexy's crew. Figuring this, he looked to where Big Sexy was and he had disappeared, leaving his AK-47 behind on the ground.

"Shit! I fucking had his ass!" Reckless cursed. He hated himself for not laying Big Sexy down when he had the chance.

Hearing someone coming from the side that the vehicles of Big Sexy's homies were approaching from, Reckless looked in that direction to see a handful of them niggaz hopping out of the cars, automatic weapons in hand. When they spotted him they opened fire on his ass. He ducked and ran, letting his AK spit fire at them as he retreated. He found cover on the side of the warehouse and whistled. Right then, his niggaz appeared from out of the shadows. They were all masked up and carrying firepower.

All hell broke loose as gunshots consumed the air and bullet shell casings deflected off the ground. Brain and skull fragments flew, and so did blood. Droplets splashed on the ground and left burgundy stains behind. Several bodies dropped as Big Sexy's and Reckless's men exchanged gunfire.

Although Reckless had lost a couple of his men, Big Sexy's niggaz were getting their asses kicked. In fact, there was only two of them niggaz left.

Reckless licked his chops as he watched his homeboys massacre the opposition. He looked to his left and saw Big Sexy duck down beside another car. He was pulling a handgun from the small of his back and checking the magazine of it to make sure it was fully loaded. Seeing that it was loaded, Reckless smacked it into the butt of his gun and cocked that bitch. He then slowly crept along the car Big Sexy was stashed beside. Looking from Big Sexy to his homeboys, Reckless saw that the giant had his sights set on them. His homeboys were so occupied with their firefight that they had neglected to watch their own backs.

"I see yo' ol' slick ass," Reckless swung out from the side of the warehouse, gripping his AK. He slowly crept upon Big Sexy. He lifted his assault rifle to spray his ass to death, but something happened that took him off guard. "Gaaah!" His eyes bulged and his mouth hung open. Blood pooled in his grill and dripped on to his gray hoodie. He looked down and saw a katana sticking halfway out of his chest. Before he knew it the ground was moving fast below him. It appeared as if he was flying but he was actually being driven.

Reckless threw his head back screaming bloody murder. He dropped his AK-47 as he was driven forward. The assault rifle went tumbling backwards on the ground hastily. Fear had come around the corner of the warehouse on his motorcycle and drew his katana. He sped towards Reckless as he was about to murder Big Sexy and thrust his katana threw his chest, driving him along on his motorcycle for a minute.

Snikttt

Fear snatched his katana from out of Reckless's chest and he fell to the ground, tumbling backwards. He then sheathed his sword and pulled out an Uzi. As he went to point his automatic weapon, the last of Big Sexy's men were being murdered. Just as the last man on Big Sexy's street team dropped dead, Fear pulled the trigger of his Uzi, waving it around. Some of the bullets shattered the windows of the vehicles that crowded the war zone, but the others met their intended targets, Reckless's men. The men hollered out in agony as bullets went through their bodies, causing them to dance on their feet. Once the last of them niggaz hit the ground, Fear stopped his motorcycle. He kicked the kickstand down with the heel of his boot and his bike leaned against it. Switching hands with his Uzi, he unsheathed his katana again. He made his way over to the men he'd shot up. The few that were still living, he finished them off, stabbing them through their hearts with his sword. Once he's stabbed the last breathing man, he did a 360, looking around to make sure not a soul among them was still alive. There wasn't, so he wiped his sword off on one of them and sheathed it at his back.

Fear looked over his shoulder and saw Big Sexy approaching him. The giant walked completely around him, looking at him in awe, touching the duds he currently had on. Fear was in a duster, Kevlar bulletproof vest, green cargo pants and boots. A bandana covered the lower half of his face to conceal his true identity. Still, Big Sexy knew his best friend. It was through his mannerisms and the look in his eyes that he was able to identify the man that had just saved his ass single handedly.

"Damn, it's really you, huh?" Big Sexy said, like he couldn't believe it was him. While he was talking Fear was busy reloading his Uzi.

Fear pulled the bandana down from the lower half of his face, looking his homeboy in his eyes. "Yeah, it's me. I got cho text. Tonight makes one year from the day I checked into those mountains. I left a changed man."

"I see." Big Sexy nodded and gave him a brotherly hug. "I missed yo' itty bitty ass, man. It's good to see you back home." He patted him on his shoulder.

"Uhhhhhhhh!" Reckless's moaning in agony drew Big Sexy's and Fear's attention. They looked over their shoulders and found him trying to pull himself up. His bloody hand grabbed the side view mirror of a nearby car and he pulled himself upon his feet. He staggered forward and fell to the ground again.

"Excuse me, but I'm gonna have to cut this lil' reunion short. I have something that warrants my undivided attention," Fear brushed past Big Sexy and headed in Reckless's direction, Uzi down at his side. When he finally found himself upon Reckless, he was lying slumped against the car he'd fallen near. Blood dripped off his chin as he held the wound in his chest with both hands. He coughed up blood and looked up to the man whose shadow eclipsed him. Spotting the Uzi down at his side, he knew he'd come to finish him off, and he was willing to accept his fate.

Fear pointed the dangerous end of his Uzi at Reckless. He was about to pull the trigger when Big Sexy touched his wrist and insisted that he did the honors. Fear obliged his homeboy and stepped aside. At this time, Big Sexy was left standing over a slumped Reckless. Seeing that this was the end for him, Reckless shut his eyelids and said a prayer, crossing himself in the sign of the holy crucifix.

Blatatat!

A quick spray of the Uzi ceased all of Reckless's movements and sent him where ever the fuck Davino went when he was murdered. Once Big Sexy had finished his enemy off, Fear took the murder weapon away from him and tossed it aside. He then motioned for him to follow him as he ran back towards his motorcycle. He mounted his bike, kicked the kickstand up and revved that mothafucka up. Afterwards, he motioned for Big Sexy to climb onto the back of the bike and passed him the helmet. Once the giant had put the helmet on, Fear sped away from the bloody crime scene, leaving smoke from his exhaust pipes in his wake.

***

The sound of Fear's speeding motorcycle filled the air as he flew up the street. He was going so fast the wind ruffled him and Big Sexy's clothing. Fear listened intently as Big Sexy filled him in on how he ended up staying in the crack game after his departure. The only detail he left out was the deal he made with Broli in order to save his ass. What the fuck did he look like telling Fear he sold him out so he could stay his black ass out of prison? There wasn't any doubt in his mind that he'd kill him as soon as he got off his motorcycle.

"What did he have on you?" Fear inquired, zipping past cars in traffic. His sights were set on the freeway and it was getting closer and closer.

"Crooked mothafucka planted a brick on me." Big Sexy told him. "He told me as long as I moved weight for 'em, I'd stay a free man. I sure as fuck wasn't going to argue with that. I had to do what I had to do to keep my ass outta the fire."

"I feel you. Ain't no shame in that."

"I'm glad you understand the position a nigga was put in."

"Of course, I would have done the same thing." Fear confessed. "I mean, shit, it ain't like you ratted a nigga out. You Griff me?"

Big Sexy was silent for a moment before he answered. "Yeah, it's a big difference."

"Look, we gotta come up with a plan to get this nigga outta our hair. I can't move how I want as long as this nigga around."

"Don't worry about 'em. He's already being taken care of."

Vroooom!

The motorcycle ripped up the street.

***

Gunplay parked his car across the street and four houses down from his destination. He threw his hood over his head and popped open the glove-box, removing a package. After shutting the glove-box, he hopped out of the car and slammed the door shut behind him. He then looked up and down the street before crossing it. He walked briskly down the sidewalk, tucking the package at the back of his sweatpants. Pushing open the gate of a white two story house, he entered the yard glancing at the car parked in the driveway. It was a BMW. This confirmed that the nigga he had come to see was indeed home. Acknowledging this, Gunplay walked upon the porch and knocked on the black iron screen door. While waiting for someone to open the door, Gunplay occasionally looked over his shoulders. Once he heard the locks of the door coming unlocked, he turned back around in time to see Broli standing before him. His muscular form filled out a wife beater and the denim jeans he was rocking were hanging slightly off his ass. Gunplay noticed his eyes were hooded and red webbed, and the stench of marijuana coming from him was overwhelming.

Broli brought a withering blunt to his mouth and sucked on the end of it. He then blew out a cloud of smoke into the young nigga'z face. Gunplay didn't bat an eyelash as the intoxicating smoke submerged him.

"Fuck is you doing here, lil' nigga? And more importantly, how the fuck you know where I lay my head at?" Broli asked in a threatening manner. Gunplay started to buck on him, but he thought better of it once he noticed the handgun in his hand.

"I got something for you. Big Sexy thought that it was imperative for you to see it." Gunplay pulled out the package and held it before Broli's eyes, wagging it.

Broli stuck the blunt into his mouth and snatched the package from Gunplay's hand, saying, "Fuck is this, a porno?"

"Nigga, you really think my black ass came all the way over here to deliver you a fucking porno? Come on now, cuz. Don't try to play me." Gunplay stuck his hands into the pockets of his hoodie.

"Bring yo' ass on in, man." He motioned for him to come inside of his house with his handgun. Once he did, he shut and locked the door behind him. Afterwards, he led Gunplay into his living room where he popped the disc inside of a DVD player and turned on the flat-screen television set. Broli sat down on the couch while Gunplay stood, hands still in the pockets of his hoodie, watching the screen.

Broli blew out a cloud of smoke and mashed out what was left of his blunt in an ashtray on the coffee table. He watched the television screen as he dangled the remote control between his legs. What was playing out on the screen before him caused his brows to wrinkle, and he looked at Gunplay eerily. He then focused back on the television. He saw Big Sexy walking away from him as he pointed a gun at Davino and shot him to death.

"Say, bruh, what the fuck is this shit?" A pissed off Broli threw the remote control at the flat-screen and cracked its monitor. He was on his feet now and pointing his gun at Gunplay. His eyebrows arched and his nose scrunched up. His jaws were clenched and throbbing. Seeing himself in the footage murdering a mothafucka had totally blown his high.

"Easy, tough guy," Gunplay said. His hands were still in the pockets of his hoodie as he stared into Broli's face. The young nigga didn't even break a sweat. It didn't appear to bother him that his life was being threatened. "You bust a cap in my ass, and the big homie gone make sure that footage gets sent to every news station in Southern California."

"That slimy fat-back fried chicken eatin' cocksucka." Broli said under his breath, still pointing his gun at Gunplay.

"Now, look, in order for this footage to stay outta the public's eye," Gunplay began. "My man is gonna need you to lay off of 'em. That means falling the fuck back and letting 'em run thangs how he's been running 'em…without yo' input of course."

"What about my cut?"

"Ain't no mo' cut, cuz. Big is severing ties with you." Gunplay told him. "And if you decide to do anything besides destroy that evidence you got on 'em, he's gonna use that footage to make you famous."

A defeated Broli lowered his handgun at his side and bowed his head, massaging the bridge of his nose. Big Sexy had a handful of his nuts and he was squeezing them. He knew if he didn't want them to rupture he'd better leave him alone.

Gunplay walked over to the coffee table and picked up the blunt that Broli was smoking earlier. He sparked up the blunt and took a few drags from it, blowing smoke into the air.

"This is some primo shit chu got here." Gunplay looked at the burning blunt. He then looked back up at Broli, "You gotta shoot me yo' connect's number, pronto, cuz."

Broli's hateful eyes darted up to Gunplay, motioning towards the door with his gun, he said, "Get the fuck outta my house."

"Say no mo'." Gunplay walked down the hallway towards the front door, taking drags of the blunt all of the way.

***

Hahn pulled up in front of his granddaughter's house and killed the engine of his vehicle. Hopping out of the car, he made his way around to the trunk and opened it with his key. He took a cautious look at his surroundings before lifting the trunk open, and grabbing the duffle bag out of it. He hoisted the strap of his duffle bag over his shoulder and shut the trunk. He stepped upon the curb and made his way towards the house, keeping a watchful eye out as he adjusted the baseball cap on his head. He straightened out the sleeve of his jacket and fixed the collar of it as he proceeded towards the house. Making it upon the porch, he lifted his fist to knock on the front door but froze his hand at it. His brows crinkled up when he saw that the front door was already cracked open. Taking note of this, he pulled out his gun and gently pushed the front door open. All of the lights were out inside of the house, but the lights from the posts lining the street illuminated the living room. This showed his granddaughter and her daughter lying on the floor of the living room, dead. His granddaughter and her daughter had been strangled to death. He could see the red bruise around their necks. They'd been strangled to death. Their eyes were bulged and their mouths were stuck open. Terror was etched across their pale faces.

"Oh, Jesus, no," Hahn let the duffle bag drop to the floor. Instantly, tears filled his eyes and his mouth quivered. His heart ached greatly. He couldn't believe what had occurred, but the evidence was lying before him. "My babies, my sweet, sweet babies…no God, don't let this be happening to me." Still holding his handgun, he crawled over to his granddaughter and her daughter and pulled them into him. Teardrops fell from his eyes as he hugged their lifeless bodies against either side of him. His entire body shuddered as the tears fell from his eyes and splashed on the carpet. Coming down from his grieving, he laid the girls down on their back and crossed their arms on their chest, making them look like they were lying in coffins. Using his hand, he brushed their eyelids shut and kissed them both on their foreheads affectionately.

Hahn wiped his dripping eyes with his finger. When he looked up from what he was doing he saw something written in red lip stick across the flat-screen's display, *Turn me on and press play.* Hahn frowned because he found this odd. He looked on either side of him until he found the remote control. He picked the remote up and turned on the television. He then activated the DVD player. As soon as he did, he came face to face with Gustavo. When Hahn saw his face his stomach twisted into knots and he started feeling nauseated. He thought he was about to throw up. Homie couldn't help the feeling that death was lingering in the air and that made his skin crawl. It also caused his killa instinct to kick in and he gripped his handgun tighter. His trigger finger itched and he couldn't wait to bust his gun.

"As of right now, I know you're experiencing the same heartache and confusion I was felt when I found Caroline dead." Gustavo said to him as tears spilled down his cheeks. His eyes were red webbed and glassy. "I don't want chu to make any mistake. I orchestrated this dreadful scene before your eyes. I had the last of your bloodline extinguished so you could feel the pain I feel every day and night." He took the time to pull his handkerchief from the pocket of his suit and dabbed his dripping eyes dry. He then went on to continue. "Tell me, Hahn, do you feel how I feel?" It was silence as Hahn stared at the television's screen, tears running down his cheeks. His eyes were pink from crying and his jaws were locked. You could see the bone structure in them. The illumination from the T.V's screen shone on him as he stood before the television holding his gun at his side. A vein pulsated at his temple and his nostrils flared. He started to open fire on the T.V, but he was curious about what else Gustavo had to say, so he stayed his trigger finger. "I thought so. I cannot begin to tell you how good that makes me feel." He smiled. "Your suffering matches my own, but we're not even until you die!" Gustavo smiled wickedly. At that moment, men wearing ski masks and bulletproof vests emerged out of nowhere. They had MP-5s and Glocks.

Noticing some of the ski mask rocking niggaz at the corner of his eye, Hahn brought his handgun up and around. He pulled his trigger and muzzle flashes illuminated his face. A couple of the ski mask wearing niggaz went down when the slugs slammed into their bulletproof vests, but the rest of them opened fire on him. He hollered out in excruciation as automatic gunfire lit his ass up. He managed to get off two more shots, both striking one of his enemies in the head, splattering their blood on the television's screen. Turning around, he dropped his handgun and retreated towards the kitchen, catching fire along the way. His blood dotted the floor and the walls as he staggered away from the bullets meant to seal his fate.

Hahn made it inside of the kitchen with bullets flying over his head, hitting the walls he was staggering beside and splintering the kitchen cupboards. Hunched over, he held his held his bleeding torso, making his way towards the backdoor of the house. His blood was pelting the kitchen's linoleum and his vision was blurry. He dropped to his knee, but he pulled himself back upon his feet. As he neared the backdoor, the masked niggaz appeared behind him. Some of them had smoking guns while others were reloading their weapons. One of them went to point his gun to finish Hahn off, but another one of them raised his hand, stopping him. With the order given, the determined shooter lowered his gun to his side. Together, the niggaz in the masks watched as Hahn retreated for his life.

Hahn had gotten ten feet from the backdoor when the last masked gunman appeared. He was carrying a long black shotgun and scowling menacingly. Before Hahn could escape his wrath, homeboy racked his shotgun and let her rip. The first blast spun Hahn around, but the second blew his ass backwards. He went sliding across the floor until he eventually came to a stop at the center of the kitchen floor. Lying on his back, Hahn blinked his eyelids repeatedly and gurgled on his own blood. Blood ran from the corners of his mouth and made small pools on either side of his head. The ski masked men looked down upon him with pity, as he lay beside the stove. They watched as he reached behind the stove, doing God only knew what. They started to smoke him but they figured he wasn't much of a threat in his condition.

The masked man that blasted on Hahn spat on the floor as he came walking inside of the kitchen, both hands on his smoking shotgun. He could see Hahn's legs sticking out beside the stove as he came around it. He licked his chops and smiled devilishly.

"Ah, there you are." The masked man welding the shotgun said. He found Hahn messing with something behind the stove. Once he kicked him in his side, he howled in pain and rolled over on his back. In one hand, he had a valve that was attached to the back of the stove. Gas escaped from the valve being loose and filled the air. In the other hand, Hahn held a Zippo lighter. Looking to the nigga that had blasted him with the shotgun, he smiled knowingly and struck the small metal ball of his lighter. A bluish yellow flame leaped to life from the lighter. As soon as the flame mingled with the gas in the air, the house exploded and sent fire roaring throughout it. Flames burst out of the windows of the house and sent broken glass out into the night's air. Shards of glass came raining down on the front lawn.

Thud! Thump! Bump!
Burning body parts landed on the front lawn.

Down the block and across the street

Lethal sat behind the wheel of his van watching the raging fire through the windshield. The reflection of Hahn's goddaughter's burning house shone on the windshield. After a minute, he started the van up, pulled out of his parking space and drove off. Gripping the steering wheel with one hand, he pulled his cell phone from out of his suit's jacket and dialed up Gustavo.

***

After he dropped Big Sexy off at home, Fear drove out to the house he shared with Italia. He parked his motorcycle in the driveway and placed the kickstand down. He then, hopped off his bike and hustled up the stairs of his home, pulling out his keys. As he sifted through his keys for the one he needed to open the front door, he suddenly stopped and listened closely. His brows furrowed as he waited to hear what he'd heard again, but when he didn't he shrugged. Thinking nothing of it, Fear opened the door of his house and pushed his way inside. As soon as he crossed the threshold his eyes bulged and he gasped. Sitting before him was Italia and his mother, Verna in chairs, gagged and bound. Standing behind them was a man wearing the same face as him, but it wasn't him. It was Malik. His eyes and posture gave him away. Realizing who the man was pointing a silenced gun to the back of Italia's head was, Fear glared up at him and squared his jaws, boasting the bone structure in his face.

"Well, well, well, look who's finally home," Malik smiled sinisterly, like there was a joke that only he knew the punch line to. "You're just in time for the fun and games, Mr. Simpson." He switched hands with the gun and reached inside of his pocket, pulling out a half of a dollar silver coin. "I'm gonna flip this coin, okay? Heads your mom's dies, heads wifey gets it. Ready? Call it in the air." He flipped the coin up in the air and it was flipping so fast that it looked like a silver blur while in motion. It landed in his palm and he smacked it down on the back of his hand. His head snapped up at Fear and he was smiling harder. "Wutchu got, homie? Heads or Tails?"

"I'm not playing your fucking games!" Fear barked on Malik. He was clenching his fists so tight that veins were running through them. His head shook slightly like it was about to erupt and he was gritting his teeth.

"Wrong! You're gonna play whether you want to or not, mothafucka! You don't get no choice in the matter." Malik spat at him with a pair of hateful eyes. "Now pick!"

Fear didn't respond. He just stood there mad dogging him.

"I said, 'pick, nigga!'"

There was still no answer.

"Fine! I'ma pick for yo' ass then, you got heads."

"I swear on my father's grave if you harm one hair on either of their heads, I'ma kill yo' ass!"

The man slowly removed his palm from the back of his other hand. Seeing what the verdict was, he smiled sinisterly again and looked up at Fear.

"Well, looks like she can kiss her ass goodbye," he took the silver dollar from his other hand and pointed his weapon at the back of the woman's head that he intended to kill.

"Malik, noooooo!" Fear called out, but it was already too late.

Tranay Adams

To Be Continued…
Fear My Gangsta 3
Coming Soon

Submission Guideline

Submit the first three chapters of your completed manuscript to ldpsubmissions@gmail.com, subject line: Your book's title. The manuscript must be in a .doc file and sent as an attachment. Document should be in Times New Roman, double spaced and in size 12 font. Also, provide your synopsis and full contact information. If sending multiple submissions, they must each be in a separate email.

Have a story but no way to send it electronically? You can still submit to LDP/Ca$h Presents. Send in the first three chapters, written or typed, of your completed manuscript to:

**LDP: Submissions Dept
Po Box 870494
Mesquite, Tx 75187**

DO NOT send original manuscript. Must be a duplicate.

Provide your synopsis and a cover letter containing your full contact information.

Thanks for considering LDP and Ca$h Presents.

Tranay Adams

BOW DOWN TO MY GANGSTA

By **Ca$h**

TORN BETWEEN TWO

By **Coffee**

BLOOD STAINS OF A SHOTTA **III**

By **Jamaica**

STEADY MOBBIN **III**

By **Marcellus Allen**

BLOOD OF A BOSS **V**

By **Askari**

LOYAL TO THE GAME **IV**

LIFE OF SIN

By **T.J. & Jelissa**

A DOPEBOY'S PRAYER **II**

By **Eddie "Wolf" Lee**

IF LOVING YOU IS WRONG… **III**

LOVE ME EVEN WHEN IT HURTS **II**

By **Jelissa**

TRUE SAVAGE **VI**

By **Chris Green**

BLAST FOR ME **III**

A BRONX TALE

By **Ghost**

ADDICTIED TO THE DRAMA **III**

By **Jamila Mathis**

LIPSTICK KILLAH **III**

CRIME OF PASSION **II**

Fear My Gangsta 2

By **Mimi**

WHAT BAD BITCHES DO **III**

KILL ZONE **II**

By **Aryanna**

THE COST OF LOYALTY **II**

By **Kweli**

SHE FELL IN LOVE WITH A REAL ONE **II**

By **Tamara Butler**

LOVE SHOULDN'T HURT **III**

RENEGADE BOYS **II**

By **Meesha**

CORRUPTED BY A GANGSTA **III**

By **Destiny Skai**

A GANGSTER'S CODE **III**

By **J-Blunt**

KING OF NEW YORK III

By **T.J. Edwards**

CUM FOR ME **IV**

By **Ca$h & Company**

GORILLAS IN THE BAY

De'Kari

THE STREETS ARE CALLING

Duquie Wilson

KINGPIN KILLAZ II

Hood Rich

STEADY MOBBIN' **III**

Marcellus Allen

SINS OF A HUSTLER

ASAD

HER MAN, MINE'S TOO **II**

Nicole Goosby

GORILLAZ IN THE BAY **II**

DE'KARI

TRIGGADALE II

Elijah R. Freeman

THE STREETS ARE CALLING **II**

Duquie Wilson

Available Now

RESTRAINING ORDER **I & II**

By **CA$H & Coffee**

LOVE KNOWS NO BOUNDARIES **I II & III**

By **Coffee**

RAISED AS A GOON I, II, III & IV

BRED BY THE SLUMS I, II, III

BLAST FOR ME I & II

ROTTEN TO THE CORE I III

By **Ghost**

LAY IT DOWN **I & II**

LAST OF A DYING BREED

BLOOD STAINS OF A SHOTTA I & II

By **Jamaica**

LOYAL TO THE GAME

LOYAL TO THE GAME II

LOYAL TO THE GAME III

By **TJ & Jelissa**

BLOODY COMMAS I & II

SKI MASK CARTEL I II & III

KING OF NEW YORK I II

By **T.J. Edwards**

IF LOVING HIM IS WRONG…I & II

LOVE ME EVEN WHEN IT HURTS

By **Jelissa**

WHEN THE STREETS CLAP BACK I & II III

By **Jibril Williams**

A DISTINGUISHED THUG STOLE MY HEART I II & III

LOVE SHOULDN'T HURT I II

RENEGADE BOYS

By **Meesha**

A GANGSTER'S CODE I & II

By J-Blunt

PUSH IT TO THE LIMIT

By **Bre' Hayes**

BLOOD OF A BOSS **I, II, III & IV**

By **Askari**

THE STREETS BLEED MURDER **I, II & III**

THE HEART OF A GANGSTA I II& III

By **Jerry Jackson**

CUM FOR ME

CUM FOR ME 2

CUM FOR ME 3

An **LDP Erotica Collaboration**

BRIDE OF A HUSTLA **I II & II**

THE FETTI GIRLS **I, II& III**

CORRUPTED BY A GANGSTA I & II

By **Destiny Skai**

WHEN A GOOD GIRL GOES BAD

By **Adrienne**

A GANGSTER'S REVENGE **I II III & IV**

THE BOSS MAN'S DAUGHTERS

THE BOSS MAN'S DAUGHTERS II

THE BOSSMAN'S DAUGHTERS III

THE BOSSMAN'S DAUGHTERS IV

THE BOSS MAN'S DAUGHTERS **V**

A SAVAGE LOVE **I & II**

BAE BELONGS TO ME

A HUSTLER'S DECEIT I, II

WHAT BAD BITCHES DO I, II

By **Aryanna**

A KINGPIN'S AMBITON

A KINGPIN'S AMBITION **II**

I MURDER FOR THE DOUGH

By **Ambitious**

TRUE SAVAGE

TRUE SAVAGE II

TRUE SAVAGE **III**

TRUE SAVAGE **IV**

TRUE SAVAGE **V**

By **Chris Green**

A DOPEBOY'S PRAYER

By **Eddie "Wolf" Lee**

THE KING CARTEL **I, II & III**

By **Frank Gresham**

THESE NIGGAS AIN'T LOYAL **I, II & III**

By **Nikki Tee**

GANGSTA SHYT **I II &III**

By **CATO**

THE ULTIMATE BETRAYAL

By **Phoenix**

BOSS'N UP **I , II & III**

By **Royal Nicole**

I LOVE YOU TO DEATH

By Destiny J

I RIDE FOR MY HITTA

I STILL RIDE FOR MY HITTA

By **Misty Holt**

LOVE & CHASIN' PAPER

By **Qay Crockett**

TO DIE IN VAIN

By **ASAD**

BROOKLYN HUSTLAZ

By **Boogsy Morina**

BROOKLYN ON LOCK I & II

By **Sonovia**

GANGSTA CITY

By **Teddy Duke**

A DRUG KING AND HIS DIAMOND I & II III

A DOPEMAN'S RICHES

HER MAN, MINE'S TOO

Tranay Adams

By Nicole Goosby

TRAPHOUSE KING **I II & III**

KINGPIN KILLAZ

By **Hood Rich**

LIPSTICK KILLAH **I, II**

CRIME OF PASSION

By **Mimi**

STEADY MOBBN' **I, II**

By **Marcellus Allen**

WHO SHOT YA **I, II**

Renta

GORILLAZ IN THE BAY

DE'KARI

TRIGGADALE

Elijah R. Freeman

GOD BLESS THE TRAPPERS I, II, III

THESE SCANDALOUS STREETS I, II, III

FEAR MY GANGSTA I, II

THESE STREETS DON'T LOVE NOBODY I, II

Tranay Adams

THE STREETS ARE CALLING

Duquie Wilson

<u>BOOKS BY LDP'S CEO, CA$H</u>

<u>TRUST IN NO MAN</u>

<u>TRUST IN NO MAN 2</u>

<u>TRUST IN NO MAN 3</u>

<u>BONDED BY BLOOD</u>

<u>SHORTY GOT A THUG</u>

<u>THUGS CRY</u>

<u>THUGS CRY 2</u>

<u>THUGS CRY 3</u>

<u>TRUST NO BITCH</u>

<u>TRUST NO BITCH 2</u>

<u>TRUST NO BITCH 3</u>

<u>TIL MY CASKET DROPS</u>

<u>RESTRAINING ORDER</u>

<u>RESTRAINING ORDER 2</u>

<u>IN LOVE WITH A CONVICT</u>

<u>Coming Soon</u>

BONDED BY BLOOD 2

BOW DOWN TO MY GANGSTA